THE FIRST MILE

A Story of Distance and Desire

by

Elliot Fife

Chapter One — New Ground

The rental van smelled like someone else's life.

Ardy Alves sat wedged between a box labeled *KITCHEN (FRAGILE)* and the passenger door, watching Maine unspool through the window. His mother drove with both hands on the wheel the way she always did when she was nervous, her knuckles not quite white but close, her chin lifted a little higher than usual. Annie Alves was the kind of woman who faced things head-on and called it optimism. Ardy had always admired that about her, even when it exhausted him.

"Exit's coming up," he said.

"I know where the exit is, Rudolfo."

She only used his full name when she was concentrating. He let it go.

Portland appeared gradually — first the water tower, then the skyline low and gray against an October sky, then the bridge over the Fore River with its view of the harbor and the islands beyond. Everything was the color of slate and cold light. It looked nothing like Queens. Queens was noise and brick and the grimy smell of the 7 train. This was something else entirely. Quieter. Older. The kind of place where a person could disappear into themselves and nobody would notice.

Ardy wasn't sure yet if that was a good thing.

* * *

The apartment was on the third floor of a yellow Victorian on Brackett Street, in a neighborhood called the

West End. The landlord, a compact man named Mr. Pelletier with a gray beard and surprising kindness in his eyes, helped them carry boxes up the narrow staircase without being asked. Annie thanked him three times. Ardy thanked him once, which was about all he could manage with a stranger.

When Mr. Pelletier left them to it, Ardy stood in the center of the living room and looked around. The floors were old hardwood, a little uneven, the kind that creaked in interesting ways. The windows were tall and let in a flat, silvery light. Someone had left a small ceramic lighthouse on the windowsill — a previous tenant, presumably — and nobody had bothered to remove it.

His mother came and stood beside him.

"It has good bones," she said.

"It has a lighthouse someone forgot."

"That's lucky." She picked it up, examined it, set it back down. "We'll keep it."

Ardy looked at her — really looked, the way he sometimes caught himself doing since his father died, as if taking inventory. She was forty-two and still beautiful in the way that surprised people, dark-haired and straight-backed, with the kind of face that gave nothing away unless she wanted it to. She had not cried when they left Queens that morning. She had made coffee, locked the door of the old apartment without looking back, and driven north for six hours through the turning leaves.

He had never once seen her cry, and he didn't know whether to be grateful or heartbroken about that.

"You okay?" he asked.

She turned and looked at him with that expression she had — warm and slightly amused and absolutely certain. "I'm fine, baby. Are *you* okay?"

"I asked first."

"And I answered." She patted his shoulder once, efficiently, the way a nurse touches things — with confidence and no wasted motion. "Go find your room. I'm going to figure out where we packed the coffee maker."

* * *

His room was at the back of the apartment, overlooking a small yard and, beyond the yard's wooden fence, a narrow alley and then the backs of other houses. Not much of a view. But when he opened the window and leaned out, he could smell the ocean — faint, salt-edged, carried in on a wind from the direction of the harbor — and something about that clean scent, so unlike anything he'd ever known in Queens, loosened a knot in his chest he hadn't realized was there.

He sat on the bare mattress and took out his phone and looked at it for a while without doing anything with it. There was a text from his high school coach, Coach Briggs, asking if he'd connected with the USM track program yet. There was nothing from anyone his own age, because there was no one his own age who would think to check on him. That wasn't self-pity. It was just the arithmetic of his life so far.

He opened his running app instead and looked at the map of Portland. The USM campus was about a mile and a half away. He could see from the satellite view that there was a track nearby. He zoomed in until he could make out the oval of it, red and precise.

Tomorrow, he decided. First thing.

He didn't know what was going to happen at this university, whether he'd find his footing or continue to drift along the edges of things as he always had. He didn't know if he'd make friends, or whether the thing he carried inside him — that low hum of want that he refused to name — would keep him as isolated here as it had in every locker room, every cafeteria, every classroom where he'd learned to look away at precisely the right moment.

What he knew was how to run.

He knew the feeling of his lungs opening up after the first quarter mile, the specific silence that descended when his body found its rhythm and his mind finally, mercifully, went quiet. He knew how to push through the burn in his legs and the doubt in his chest and come out the other side of a mile feeling, briefly, like himself.

That was enough. That was a place to start.

From the kitchen came the sound of his mother humming something under her breath — an old song, something she'd sung when he was small — and the smell of coffee beginning to drift down the hallway.

Ardy lay back on the bare mattress and looked at the ceiling and breathed in the salt air coming through the open window.

Portland, he thought. *Okay. Here we go.*

* * *

Chapter Two — The Bleachers

He was out the door by six.

The city was still mostly asleep, the streets of the West End quiet except for the occasional car and the distant complaint of a gull somewhere toward the water. Ardy ran in the street rather than on the sidewalk, the way he always did when traffic allowed — the asphalt had a better give to it, easier on the joints — and he kept his pace deliberately slow, just loosening up, letting Portland come to him one block at a time.

Because the University of Southern Maine had no outdoor running track on its Portland campus, the athletes used Fitzpatrick Stadium, a city-owned facility nearby. It came into view after about a mile and a half of running north from Brackett Street — before the campus and the Deering Avenue bridge that connected the two.

Red all-weather surface, eight lanes, the outer ones slightly faded from years of sun. The infield was a well-worn rectangle of artificial turf with a long jump pit at the far end. The bleachers ran along the home straight — aluminum, twelve rows deep, the kind that rang like a bell when you climbed them.

Someone was sitting in the fifth row.

Ardy hadn't expected that. He stood at the gate and squinted. It was a girl, he thought, though at this distance and in this light he couldn't be entirely sure — chin-length dark curly hair, a dark jacket, knees drawn up, something in her lap that might have been a book. She appeared to be completely absorbed in whatever she was reading. She did not look up.

He pushed open the gate, which announced him with a long metallic groan, and she still didn't look up.

He stretched at the edge of the track for a few minutes — hip flexors, hamstrings, the left calf that always tightened overnight — and then he ran. Just easy laps to start, getting a feel for the surface, finding the line. The air was cold enough to see his breath and it tasted of salt and something faintly woodsy he couldn't identify. Maine air, he supposed. He'd have to get used to it.

He was on his fourth lap, beginning to push, when a voice called down from the bleachers.

"You pronate on the left."

Ardy startled so badly he nearly clipped the inside line. He slowed and looked up. The girl was watching him now, book closed in her lap, chin resting on her folded arms across her knees. Green eyes. The ends of her dark hair were frosted bright pink, he could see now — an inch or two of bubblegum at the tips.

"What?" he said.

"Your left foot. It rolls inward when you're tired. You're not tired yet, but it's there. Little bit."

Ardy looked down at his feet, which was not very useful while standing still. "How long have you been watching me?"

"Since you came in." She said it without any apology whatsoever. "I like watching people run. It tells you things."

"What does it tell you about me?"

She considered him with the frank, unhurried attention of someone who was genuinely thinking about it.

"That you're good. That you've been coached. That you run alone a lot." She paused. "That you're new."

"To the track?"

"To Portland."

He looked at her. "How do you get *new to Portland* from the way I run?"

"I don't." She held up the book — he could see now it was a slim paperback, a poetry collection, though he couldn't make out the title. "I've been coming here every morning for two weeks and I've never seen you before. Simple." She tilted her head. "Are you going to come up here or are you going to keep yelling at me from down there?"

He hesitated for exactly one second, then walked to the bleachers and climbed. She watched him the whole way up without any self-consciousness at all, which he found simultaneously unnerving and oddly refreshing. He sat two rows below her, sideways on the bench so he could look up at her easily, which felt like the right distance for strangers.

"Hi," she said.

"Hi."

"I'm Mack."

"Ardy."

She raised an eyebrow. "Ardy."

"Short for Rudolfo. My dad — " He stopped, then decided to continue. It was early in the morning and she had a kind face and somehow the cold air made honesty feel easier. "My dad started calling me Ardy when I was little. The R and the D in Rudolfo. It stuck."

Something shifted in her expression — not pity, which he would have hated, but a kind of careful attentiveness. "That's a good nickname," she said. "The kind that means something."

"Yeah."

She let the silence sit for a moment, which impressed him — most people rushed to fill it. Then she said: "What are you reading these days?"

He blinked. "What?"

"Books. What are you reading?"

"I — nothing, right now. I just moved in yesterday."

"So today you should go to Longfellow Books on Monument Square. It's about a ten-minute walk from here, they open at ten." She said this with the breezy authority of someone who had strong opinions and no particular anxiety about sharing them. "What do you like?"

"I don't know. Whatever. History, sometimes."

"History." She nodded slowly, as if filing this away. "Okay. What else?"

"Why are you — " He shook his head, almost laughing. "You don't even know me."

"That's the point," she said simply. "What else?"

He thought about it. The cold air came off the infield in a long, slow wave. Somewhere across the campus a door banged shut. "I like things that make sense," he said finally, which wasn't really an answer to her question but seemed to satisfy her anyway.

"What are you studying?"

"Engineering. Probably."

"Probably," she repeated, catching the hedge. "I'm doing health and clinical sciences. I want to be a therapist. For kids, maybe." She paused. "Don't tell me that surprises you."

"It doesn't," he said, and meant it.

She smiled then — a sudden, full smile that rearranged her whole face. "Good answer." She uncurled herself slightly and held out the paperback toward him. "Have you read Anne Carson?"

He took it. *Autobiography of Red.* He turned it over and read the back without really absorbing any of it. "No."

"You should. She does this thing where mythology and real life just, like — collapse into each other. It sounds weird. It's not weird." She took it back. "She's from Canada originally."

"Is that relevant?"

"Everything is relevant." She said it without irony, which somehow made it funnier. "Where are you from?"

"Queens."

"New York." She nodded. "I'm from Providence. So we're both transplants." She looked out at the track, then back at him. "It's a good place to land, I think. Portland. It feels like a city that's still figuring itself out, you know? I like that."

Ardy looked out at the red oval below them, the empty lanes, the long jump pit with its raked sand pale as beach in the early light. He thought about the ceramic lighthouse on the windowsill of the apartment. He thought about his mother's humming.

"Yeah," he said. "Maybe."

Mack opened her book again, which he understood to mean the interrogation was over, at least for now. He sat there for another minute, not quite ready to go back to running, not quite sure what had just happened. He'd had conversations with strangers before, obviously. But not like this — not this quickly, not with this sense of the ground shifting beneath him in a way that felt, strangely, like relief.

"You going to run more?" she asked without looking up.

"Yeah."

"Your left foot," she said. "Think about the big toe pushing down. Corrects the pronation."

He climbed back down the bleachers and returned to the track. He ran four more laps, and on each one he thought about his left foot, and on each one it was a little better. When he finally stopped, breathing hard, hands on his knees, he glanced back up at the bleachers.

Mack was reading, pink hair tips catching the first pale light of morning, completely unbothered.

He found himself smiling on the walk home.

* * *

Chapter Three — The Team

The email from Coach Dubé had arrived three days before Ardy left Queens.

It was brief and businesslike — welcome to the program, first practice Tuesday at four, bring your spikes, don't be late. Ardy had read it four times, then saved it to a folder he'd labeled *USM* and tried not to think about it too much. Thinking about things too much was a habit he was trying to break, with mixed results.

Tuesday came anyway, the way Tuesdays do.

* * *

He arrived at Fitzpatrick Stadium twelve minutes early, which he figured was the right amount of early — not so early that he looked desperate, not so close to four that he seemed indifferent. He changed into his spikes sitting on the lowest bench of the bleachers, fingers moving through the familiar routine of lacing, double-knotting, checking the left one twice because it always came loose.

There were already six or seven other guys on the infield, stretching or jogging easy laps, talking in the loose comfortable way of people who knew each other. Ardy watched them from the bleachers for a moment. There was a particular kind of social geometry to a new team — the clusters, the pairs, the one or two people off on their own — and he had learned over the years to read it quickly, to find where he might fit without anyone having to make room.

He was good at making himself small. He was less good at deciding whether that was a useful skill or just a sad one.

He came down to the infield and began stretching near the outside of the group, close enough to be part of it, far enough to not impose. He noticed, without particular surprise, that he was the shortest guy out there — compact where the others were rangy, slight where they were broad. His father had been the same way, built for speed rather than scale. A couple of guys nodded at him. He nodded back. A wiry sophomore named Marcus introduced himself, said Coach Dubé was good, tough but fair, and that the jumpers — the long jumpers and high jumpers who shared the infield — were annoying but you got used to them. Ardy smiled at that, and Marcus seemed satisfied and jogged off.

That was the thing about track people, he'd always found. They were easier than most. The sport sorted you by event and then mostly left you alone, which suited him fine.

He was working through his hip flexors, one knee on the cold rubber surface, when he became aware of someone arriving on the far side of the track.

He didn't look up right away. He finished the stretch, switched sides, and then — without entirely meaning to — looked up.

A guy had come through the far gate and was moving along the back straight at an easy jog, just warming up, not pushing at all. He was tall, broad-shouldered, with the kind of build that looked powerful even at rest — a runner's leanness through the hips and legs but genuine strength in the shoulders and chest. Ginger hair, cut short. Even from this distance, in the flat afternoon light, there was something about the way he moved that was hard not to watch — and in one brief unguarded glance at his face, something clean and open in it even in profile, Ardy felt a small unfamiliar pull somewhere deep and unnameable that he shut down before it became anything. Fluid and unhurried, like someone who had long ago made peace with the fact that his body knew what it was doing.

Ardy looked away.

He switched to his hamstring stretch, forehead toward his knee, eyes on the ground. His heart was doing something he didn't particularly appreciate.

Stop it, he told himself. It wasn't even a thought so much as a reflex — the automatic hand that reached for the door handle before the door could open. He'd had years of practice at it by now. See something, feel something, shut it down, move on. The sequence took about three seconds and he'd gotten very efficient at it.

He stood up and shook out his legs and focused on the far end of the track where a man in a USM Athletics jacket was setting up cones. Coach Dutil, the assistant — fifties, weathered face, clipboard, the particular no-nonsense posture of someone who had been standing on tracks for thirty years and intended to stand on them for thirty more. Coach Dubé, he'd been told, ran the program from the office and showed up to meets. Dutil ran practice. That division of labor, Ardy thought, probably suited everyone just fine.

"Alves."

He turned. Dutil was looking at him from across the infield, not unkindly, but with the evaluating squint of a man who had seen a thousand freshmen and could tell in about thirty seconds which ones were worth his time.

"Yes, sir."

"Lane four. Let me see your eight hundred."

Just like that. No preamble, no introduction to the group, no ceremony. Ardy appreciated it more than he could have explained.

He went to lane four and shook out his arms and settled into his stance. A couple of the other athletes drifted over to watch — casually, the way runners watched each other, with technical interest and no particular sentiment. He was peripherally aware of the ginger-haired guy somewhere off to the left, no longer jogging, apparently watching too. He pushed that awareness down firmly and looked at the track ahead of him.

Dutil raised a hand. "Go."

Ardy went.

The first two hundred he ran controlled, finding the pace, letting the surface come up to meet him. The back straight was into a slight headwind and he tucked his chin and shortened his stride and pushed through it. Coming off the final bend his legs were burning cleanly, the good kind of burn, the kind that meant everything was working the way it was supposed to, and he opened up his stride down the home straight and crossed the finish with his lungs wide open and his whole body singing with effort.

He slowed to a jog, hands behind his head, breathing hard.

Dutil looked at his stopwatch for a moment. Then he looked at Ardy with an expression that was not quite a smile but was adjacent to one.

"Lane two," he said. "Do it again."

Ardy laughed — a short, breathless sound — and went to lane two.

* * *

Practice lasted ninety minutes. By the end of it he knew a few more names — Marcus, the sophomore miler who ran like he was angry at the ground; Derek, a lanky junior hurdler who kept cracking jokes nobody laughed at except himself; a quiet freshman named Paul who ran the mile and seemed about as comfortable with small talk as Ardy was. He did not learn the ginger-haired guy's name.

After practice he sat on the bleachers again and changed out of his spikes and back into his trainers, fingers working through the familiar routine in reverse. The stadium was emptying out, athletes heading off in twos and threes, the low murmur of conversation fading.

"Good eight hundred."

Ardy looked up.

The ginger-haired guy was standing at the end of his row, kit bag over one shoulder, looking at him with an easy friendliness that seemed to cost him nothing at all. Up close his eyes were a clear, light blue, the kind of blue that made you think of cold water. There was a dusting of freckles across his nose and cheekbones. He was smiling slightly, and it made something in him seem even more open than it already was.

Ardy's heart did the thing again.

"Thanks," he said. His voice came out level, which he was grateful for.

"I'm James," the guy said. "James Rhys. Junior. Fifteen hundred, five thousand."

"Ardy Alves. Freshman. Eight hundred, mile."

James nodded, still with that easy smile. "Where are you from?"

"Queens."

"Long way." He said it without making it a big deal, which Ardy appreciated. "You settling in okay?"

"Getting there."

James shifted his kit bag on his shoulder. "A few of us usually go to Bayside after practice on Tuesdays if you want to come. It's just a diner, nothing special. Good coffee."

Ardy looked at him. The offer was friendly and uncomplicated and there was nothing in James Rhys's clear blue eyes except ordinary human warmth, and Ardy knew — with a certainty that sat in his stomach like a stone — that he should say yes, that this was exactly the kind of moment that normal people navigated without drama.

"Maybe next week," he said. "Still getting unpacked."

Something flickered across James's face — not offense, just a mild, passing curiosity — and then the easy smile returned. "Sure. Next week." He lifted a hand in a small wave. "Good running, Ardy."

He walked off down the bleachers and out through the gate, kit bag swaying, and Ardy sat there for another minute looking at the empty track.

The cones were still out on the infield from practice. The light was going flat and gray. Somewhere in the distance a car horn sounded twice.

He tied his trainers carefully. He did not let himself think about anything.

He ran home.

* * *

Chapter Four — The Witch of Deering Avenue

It started, as many things did with Mack, with a question he wasn't prepared for.

They were sitting in McGoldrick two weeks into the semester, Ardy with a coffee and a differential equations problem set, Mack with a green tea and a copy of Euripides in the original Greek, which she read the way other people read the back of a cereal box — casually, without apparent effort, occasionally making a small disapproving noise at something Euripides had done.

"Do you have a sweetheart?" she asked, without looking up.

Ardy's pencil stopped moving. "A what?"

"A sweetheart." She turned a page. "Girlfriend. Boyfriend. Person you're gone on. Whatever the applicable term is."

He felt the warmth rise in his face and was grateful she wasn't looking at him. "No," he said. "That hasn't — no."

"Hm." She made the same noise she'd been making at Euripides.

"What does *hm* mean?"

"It means hm." She closed the book, finally, and looked at him with those frank green eyes that always made him feel slightly transparent, like she could see the wiring behind the walls. "You've been here three weeks. You know one person."

"I know you."

"You know one person," she repeated. "You go to practice, you go home, you study, you run in the morning. You have coffee with me on Tuesdays and Thursdays."

"I like Tuesdays and Thursdays."

"Ardy." She said his name the way his mother sometimes did — not unkindly, but with a weight to it, like she was setting something down on a table between them. "When's the last time you let yourself want something?"

The question landed somewhere below his sternum and sat there. He looked at his problem set. The equations looked back at him, indifferent and clean, which he appreciated about mathematics — it never asked you anything you weren't equipped to answer.

"I want to finish this problem set," he said.

Mack was quiet for a moment. Then: "You know I'm a witch."

He looked up. "You've mentioned it."

"I have powers," she said, with complete serenity. "Perception. Insight. The ability to arrange circumstances in ways that appear coincidental but are not." She picked up her green tea. "Tomorrow. Meet me at your locker after lunch."

"Why?"

She smiled — that sudden, full smile that rearranged her face. "Because I said so. And because your secret love is about to appear."

"My — " He shook his head. "Mack."

"Twelve thirty," she said, and opened her Euripides again. "Don't be late."

* * *

He almost didn't go.

He stood outside McGoldrick at twelve twenty-five telling himself it was a ridiculous errand, that Mack was winding him up, that whatever she had planned was going to be embarrassing and he should just go to the library instead and spend the hour productively.

He went.

His locker was on the second floor of the humanities building, a narrow corridor that smelled of old carpet and radiator heat. Mack was already there when he arrived, leaning against the lockers with her arms folded and the expression of someone who had just successfully completed phase one of a plan and was very pleased about it.

"You came," she said.

"I was in the neighborhood."

"Your locker is on the second floor of a building you have no classes in."

"I was in the neighborhood," he said again, and she grinned.

He worked his combination and opened the locker and stood there pretending to look for something he didn't need. His heart was doing its inconvenient thing again, though he couldn't entirely have explained why. The corridor was quiet, just the distant sound of a door closing somewhere below, the tick of a pipe in the wall.

Then footsteps on the stairs.

Mack straightened slightly, which was the only warning he got.

"Hey," she called out.

Ardy turned around.

The broad-shouldered, ginger-haired guy coming down the corridor was tall — taller than Ardy by several inches, which was not unusual, but James's height had a

particular quality to it, easy and unassuming, like he'd
never once thought to use it against anyone. It took Ardy
approximately half a second to recognize him as the same
person he'd been carefully not thinking about for two
weeks. James Rhys, in a grey USM hoodie and dark jeans
that did nothing to discourage attention, a backpack slung
over one shoulder, looking slightly puzzled in the friendly
way of someone who had agreed to something without
being entirely sure what it was.

His eyes found Mack first, then moved to Ardy.

Something passed across his face — just a flicker,
quick as a blink, there and gone — and then the easy smile
arrived, the one that made his eyes seem to smile too, and
Ardy felt the floor do something it wasn't supposed to do.

The textbook he'd been holding hit the ground. Then
the notebook on top of it. Then his pencil, which rolled
with dedicated purpose toward the opposite wall.

"Oh — " Ardy crouched for them at the same moment
James did, and for one lurching second they were both
down there on the floor of the corridor, and James
gathered up the textbook and the notebook in one easy
motion and held them out, and Ardy took them, and their
fingers didn't quite touch but almost, almost, and James
was close enough that Ardy could see the individual
freckles across the bridge of his nose.

They both stood up.

"Thanks," Ardy said. His voice came out level, which
felt like a minor miracle.

"No problem." James handed the pencil back too,
without making anything of it, as if people dropped their
books in front of him every day and he was simply glad to
help.

He turned back to his locker and stared at it.

"Hey," James said. His voice was even better up close than it had been across a track, warm and unhurried, with a slight lilt to it that Ardy couldn't place. Welsh, maybe — some distant inheritance. "Mack said to come find her here. I wasn't sure what floor — "

"Second floor," Mack said. "You found it. James, this is Ardy. Ardy — James." She gestured between them with the casual authority of a diplomat concluding a treaty. "Ardy's new in town and you guys are both like total track rabbits, so." She shrugged. "Just wanted you two to meet."

Ardy turned back from his locker. He made himself look at James directly, which took a small but genuine act of will.

"Hey," he said. "We've actually met. Sort of. Practice."

"Right!" James pointed at him, and his face opened up with recognition. "Eight hundred. Coach Dutil made you run it twice."

"Yeah."

"That was a good eight hundred."

"You said that already," Ardy said, and then immediately wondered why he'd said that.

But James just laughed — an easy, unguarded sound — and Ardy felt something loosen slightly in his chest, against his better judgment. "Fair enough." He shifted his backpack on his shoulder. "You settling in okay? You said you were still unpacking last time."

"Mostly settled now."

"Good." He nodded, and there was nothing in his expression except ordinary friendliness, the same warmth Ardy had noticed at practice, the same quality of paying actual attention when he asked a question, as if the answer genuinely mattered to him. It was disarming in a way that

Ardy resented slightly, because it made the whole situation considerably harder to manage. "Mack says you're an engineering student."

Ardy glanced at Mack, who was studying the ceiling with elaborate innocence. "Probably engineering."

"Probably," James said, catching it the same way Mack had. "What else are you considering?"

"I don't know yet." He paused. "What are you studying?"

"Education. I want to teach." He said it without any self-consciousness, which Ardy noted. Some guys got weird about saying they wanted to be teachers, as if it required defending. James just said it, flat and sure. "Secondary school, maybe. English."

"That's — " Ardy searched for the right word and landed on: "That suits you."

Something shifted in James's expression — just briefly, just enough — and then he blushed. A clean, sudden color in his fair cheeks that he seemed to become aware of almost immediately, and Ardy watched him will it away with what was clearly long and weary practice.

"Thanks," James said, and looked at his watch. "I've got a seminar at one but — we should run together sometime. If you want."

"Sure," Ardy said.

"Good." The easy smile again. He lifted a hand toward Mack. "Thanks for the introduction, MacKenzie."

"It's Mack," she said.

"Right. Mack." He said it with a small, warm amusement, and then he was gone back down the corridor, footsteps fading on the stairs.

Ardy stood at his open locker for a moment. Then he closed it, slowly, and turned to look at Mack.

She was already looking at him, green eyes bright, the ghost of a smile at the corner of her mouth.

"Don't," he said.

"I didn't say anything."

"You were about to."

She held up both hands in a gesture of pure innocence that convinced neither of them. Then she picked up her bag from the floor and slung it over her shoulder and began walking toward the stairs.

"Tuesdays and Thursdays," she said, without turning around. "And maybe branch out a little."

He stood in the empty corridor for another moment, alone with the tick of the pipe in the wall and the distant sounds of the building going about its day.

His heart was doing the thing.

He let it, just for a second.

Then he shouldered his own bag and went to his next class.

* * *

Chapter Five — Parallel Lines

James had said *sometime* and Ardy had assumed that meant eventually, vaguely, in the way that college people said *we should hang out* and meant absolutely nothing by it.

He did not assume this for long.

The text came two days later, Thursday evening, while Ardy was eating cereal over his differential equations and half-listening to his mother on the phone in the next room, her voice low and warm the way it got when she was talking to someone she liked.

Hey it's James Rhys. Mack gave me your number hope that's ok. Running tomorrow morning? 6am Fitzpatrick?

Ardy read it three times. Then he put his phone face-down on the table and ate another spoonful of cereal and looked at his equations.

Then he picked up the phone and typed: *Sure. See you there.*

He put the phone down again. From the next room his mother laughed at something, that full easy laugh she'd always had, the one his father used to say could fix a bad day at fifty paces. Ardy looked at his equations. He thought about freckles across the bridge of a nose, close enough to count. He thought about the word *almost*.

He picked up his pencil and got back to work.

* * *

James was already there when Ardy arrived, stretching against the gate in the gray pre-dawn, breath visible in the cold air. He was wearing a dark blue long-sleeve and track pants and looked, Ardy noted with the detached clinical objectivity he was working very hard to maintain, completely unreasonably good for six in the morning.

"Hey," James said, straightening.

"Hey."

"Sleep okay?"

"Fine. You?"

"Always." He said it with a simple contentment, like someone who had never once lain awake cataloguing his own thoughts. Ardy envied him this in a way that was almost fond. "You want to set the pace or should I?"

"You set it," Ardy said. "I'll tell you if you're going too slow."

James looked at him for a moment, and then that smile arrived — not the full easy one but something smaller and more private, the kind that didn't necessarily mean to be seen. "Okay," he said. "Let's go."

* * *

The first half mile James ran easy, getting a feel for the surface and the cold, and Ardy ran beside him and said nothing and felt the familiar machinery of his body engage — lungs opening, legs finding their rhythm, the particular mental quiet that running always brought settling over him like a hand on the back of his neck.

He'd always run alone. He hadn't expected running beside someone to feel like anything in particular.

It felt like something.

There was a quality to James's stride — long and controlled, economical in the way of experienced distance runners — that set a kind of tempo Ardy's body responded to without being asked. They weren't matching each other exactly, their gaits were too different for that, Ardy's stride shorter and quicker against James's long reach, but there was a rhythm between them nonetheless. Call and response. Two instruments in the same key.

James pushed the pace slightly coming off the first bend and Ardy went with him without comment, and he felt rather than saw James register this — a small adjustment, a recalibration, the way a runner responds to discovering that the person beside them is better than expected.

Good, Ardy thought, with a satisfaction that had nothing complicated in it. Just that. Good.

They ran four laps without speaking. The sky went from black to a deep charcoal gray, and the stadium lights threw long shadows across the track, and their breath came in matching clouds in the cold air. Somewhere beyond the stadium walls Portland was beginning its day — the distant sound of a truck, a dog barking once and stopping, the first tentative birds.

On the fifth lap James said, without turning his head: "You run alone a lot."

It wasn't a question. Ardy glanced at him sideways. "What makes you say that?"

"You run like someone who's used to setting their own pace. Took you about two laps to stop compensating for me."

Ardy considered this. "Is that a criticism?"

"Observation." A beat. "I run alone a lot too."

"You're the most popular guy on the team."

"That doesn't mean anything," James said, and there was something in his voice — just a thread of it, quickly gone — that made Ardy look at him again. But James's face was forward, composed, giving nothing away. "Popular just means people know your name. It's not the same as anything else."

They ran another half lap in silence.

"What's the something else?" Ardy asked.

James was quiet long enough that Ardy thought he wasn't going to answer. Then he said: "People knowing which version of you is the real one, I guess." He said it lightly, like it was nothing, like he was talking about the weather. "Anyway." He pushed the pace again, more significantly this time, and Ardy felt the shift in his own legs and matched it, and whatever had briefly opened between them closed again, neatly, and they ran.

* * *

Eight laps. Ardy lost count of the time somewhere in the middle and didn't care. His legs were burning cleanly and his lungs were fully open and the cold air tasted of salt and the coming winter and he was, he realized with a mild surprise, happy. Not the careful, managed happiness of getting through a day successfully, but something simpler and less considered — the animal happiness of a body doing what it was built for, in good company, on a quiet morning.

They slowed together at the end of the eighth lap, instinctively, neither of them calling it — they just both knew. Ardy put his hands on his knees and breathed. James walked a slow circle with his hands behind his head, chest heaving.

"Good," James said, between breaths.

"Yeah."

They walked a cool-down lap side by side, not talking much, the silence easy in the way that silences between runners often were — the shared exhaustion making everything simpler. Ardy's left foot was pronating again, he could feel it, and he thought about Mack's voice from the bleachers: *think about the big toe pushing down.* He corrected it without breaking stride.

At the gate James stopped and bent to check his laces. Ardy waited, which he did without thinking about it, and then thought about it, and then decided not to.

"Same time next week?" James said, straightening.

"Sure," Ardy said. "Or earlier if you want."

James looked at him. The gray morning light was turning slowly golden at the edges, catching the ginger in his hair, and there was a smear of cold color in his cheeks from the run. Standing this close Ardy was aware, as he always was, of how much taller James was — the easy, unassuming height of him, solid and warm against the cold morning air — and he made himself look up at James's face rather than away, which took the usual small act of will. He looked, Ardy thought, like someone painted by a person who was very good at painting and who had also been showing off a little.

He looked away.

"Earlier works," James said. "I'll text you."

"Okay."

James lifted a hand — that same small wave from the practice bleachers — and headed off toward the campus bridge. Ardy stood at the gate and watched him go, just for a second, just long enough, and then turned and ran home the long way, through streets that were just beginning to fill with the ordinary morning, and let himself think about nothing whatsoever, which was becoming something he was increasingly bad at.

* * *

Chapter Six — What Mack Knows

It was a Thursday, which meant coffee, which meant Mack.

They had settled into a routine — Tuesdays and Thursdays, McGoldrick, nine o'clock, the corner table by the window that looked out onto the quad. Mack was always there first. Ardy had tested this theory three times now by arriving progressively earlier, and each time Mack had already been there, green tea in hand, reading something formidable. He had given up trying to beat her and accepted it as one of the fixed laws of his new universe.

It was the second week of November and the quad outside was doing its best impression of a Maine winter — bare trees, iron-gray sky, the first serious suggestion of snow in the air. Students crossed it quickly with their chins tucked, coats pulled tight. Ardy watched them through the window and wrapped both hands around his coffee and felt, with some surprise, that he was glad to be on the inside.

Portland was beginning, slowly and without fanfare, to feel like somewhere he lived.

"How was the run this morning?" Mack asked, without looking up from her book. It was Sappho today — the Greek again, the slim volume she carried everywhere.

"Good. Cold."

"James?"

"He was there."

She turned a page. "And?"

"And we ran." He looked at her. "That's what running is, Mack. You go around the track. Repeatedly."

"I know what running is." She set her book down and looked at him with that clear, unhurried attention. "I'm asking about James."

"I just told you about James."

"You told me he was there." She picked up her tea. "That's not the same thing."

Ardy looked out the window. A guy was crossing the quad with an umbrella that the wind immediately turned inside out, and he stood there for a moment looking at it with profound resignation before folding it up and walking on. Ardy felt a certain kinship with him.

"He's a good runner," he said.

"Ardy."

"He's going to go sub-four in the mile by spring, I think. His form is — "

"Ardy."

He stopped. He looked at her. She was watching him with an expression he hadn't seen from her before — still warm, still Mack, but with something underneath it that was careful and serious and very still.

"I'm not going to make this weird," she said quietly. "I just want you to know that I see you. Okay? That's all. I see you and it's completely fine and it will always be completely fine and you don't have to say anything or do anything or be anything other than exactly what you already are."

McGoldrick went about its business around them — the hiss of the espresso machine, a burst of laughter from a table across the room, the scrape of a chair. Ardy looked at his coffee. He turned the cup slowly in his hands.

"Mack — "

"You don't have to say anything," she said again. Firmly, but gently. "I mean it. I'm not asking you for anything. I just — " She paused, choosing her words with an unusual care. "I know what it's like to carry something around that you don't have a name for yet. Or maybe you have a name for it and the name is the scary part. Either way." She lifted her tea and held it close to her face, letting the steam rise, the way someone might before saying something they'd been thinking about for a while. "You don't have to carry it alone. That's the only thing I'm saying."

Ardy was quiet for a long moment.

Outside, the first snow began — tentative and exploratory, just a few flakes, the sky testing the idea. One landed on the window glass and held its shape for a moment before dissolving.

"I don't know what I am," he said finally. His voice came out lower than he intended, and very even, the way his voice got when he was being more honest than he'd planned. "I mean — I have thoughts. About — " He stopped. Started again. "I've always just shut it down before it becomes anything. It's easier."

"Easier than what?"

He thought about it seriously, the way the question deserved. "Easier than being something that makes everything harder."

Mack was quiet. She didn't rush to fill the silence or offer him a tidy reframe or tell him it didn't have to be hard — all the things a lesser person might have said. She just sat with him in it for a moment, which was exactly right.

"Okay," she said at last. "Can I say one thing?"

"You're going to say it anyway."

"One thing," she said. "And then we can talk about James's mile time or whatever you want." She leaned forward slightly. "You're one of the most genuinely good people I've met. And whatever you are — whatever the name turns out to be, or isn't — that doesn't, like, change a single thing about you that matters."

Ardy looked at her for a moment. This girl he'd known for six weeks, who read ancient Greek for fun and called herself a witch and had somehow, without asking permission, become the most important person in his daily life.

"You're very strange," he said.

"Wildly," she agreed.

"I'm glad I met you."

Something shifted in her face — just briefly, a kind of warmth that was surprised by itself. Then the usual Mack settled back over it, composed and faintly amused. "Obviously," she said. "I'm delightful." She picked up her Sappho. "Now. James's mile time."

Ardy laughed — a real one, the kind that came from somewhere uncomplicated.

Mack lowered her book and stared at him with theatrical astonishment. "Was that — did you just — " She pressed a hand to her chest. "I need a moment. I just heard Ardy Alves laugh. An actual laugh. Out loud. In public."

"Stop."

"I'm not sure I can. This is historic." She looked around the room as if seeking witnesses. "Someone should mark this on a calendar."

"Mack."

"I'm just saying." She raised her book again, failing entirely to suppress her grin. "It's a good laugh. You should use it more."

He shook his head, still smiling despite himself. "James ran a 4:08 at the last practice time trial. Dutil thinks he can get to 3:58 by conference."

"Is that good?"

"It's very good."

"Hm." She turned a page. "Almost as good as having excellent taste in friends."

Ardy shook his head and drank his coffee and looked out at the snow, which was coming more steadily now, covering the quad in a thin white quiet, and felt something in his chest that was not happiness exactly but was closer to it than he'd been in a long time.

* * *

Chapter Seven — Orbit

It happened gradually, the way most things that matter do.

By the third week of November they were running together every Tuesday and Friday morning, six o'clock, at the stadium. By the fourth week James had started texting the night before — nothing much, just a confirmation, sometimes a weather report delivered with dry commentary (*28 degrees tomorrow. Wear something that doesn't hate you*), and Ardy would read these in bed before sleeping and feel something he'd become practiced at not examining too closely.

He examined it anyway, sometimes, in the quiet before sleep — turning it over carefully, the way you might handle something fragile you weren't sure belonged to you.

* * *

The runs themselves had developed their own grammar.

The first mile they didn't talk. This had never been discussed; it had simply emerged, the way the right things sometimes did when two people paid attention to each other without meaning to. The first mile was for settling in — finding the rhythm, letting the cold air do its work, shaking off whatever the night had left behind. Ardy had always needed that first mile to himself, mentally, and somewhere in their second or third run he had registered with a quiet surprise that James seemed to need it too.

There were other things he registered during that first mile, when there was nothing to do but run and notice. The way James's breath came in a steady, unhurried rhythm even at pace. The fact that he smelled, faintly, of something clean and warm that Ardy couldn't quite name — something like cut grass or cedarwood, carried on cold air, there and gone when the wind shifted. He noticed it once and told himself he hadn't, and noticed it again the next week and gave up pretending.

After the first mile, they talked.

Not about anything important, mostly. James had strong opinions about coffee — he was particular about it in a way that Ardy found oddly endearing — and would sometimes spend a quarter lap describing the specific failures of whatever café's brew he'd drunk that morning. Ardy discovered he had opinions about mathematics that he'd never had occasion to share with anyone before, and James listened to these with genuine interest, asking questions that were sometimes surprisingly good for someone who described himself as a words person, not a numbers person.

"But why does it matter if it's elegant?" James asked one morning, breath clouding in the cold air. "If it works, it works."

"Because an inelegant proof is like — " Ardy searched for an analogy that would land. "It's like running with bad form. You get to the finish line but you've wasted energy and stressed things that didn't need stressing and a better version existed."

James was quiet for a few strides, considering this. "Okay," he said. "I actually get that."

"I know you do."

James glanced at him sideways. "Was that a compliment?"

"It was an observation."

"From you," James said, "I'll take it."

* * *

There were other things too, outside the track.

James appeared at the library table where Ardy studied on Wednesday afternoons — the third floor, the window overlooking the quad, the chair Ardy had claimed by virtue of consistent occupation. James didn't make a production of it, just set his bag down across the table from Ardy and took out his books and worked. Ardy worked too, and two hours passed in a companionable silence that Ardy would not have been able to explain to anyone who asked why it felt significant.

They ate lunch together twice, then three times, in the dining hall — a round table near the window that James seemed to gravitate toward, and Ardy found himself gravitating toward too. Marcus from the track team joined them sometimes, and a tall quiet guy named Owen who was James's roommate and spoke rarely but observantly, and occasionally other people whose names Ardy gathered slowly, like stones from a riverbed.

He was, he realized one afternoon with a mild shock, accumulating a life.

It was not a dramatic realization. It arrived the way November light did — low and slanted. He was sitting at his usual library table, James across from him deep in what appeared to be a very troubling essay about Romantic poetry, frowning at it with an expression of personal affront. His hands were flat on either side of the open book — broad, smooth, very still, the hands of someone comfortable in their own body — and Ardy looked at them for a moment longer than he meant to before looking back at his problem set.

He kept working. Or tried to.

A few minutes passed. He looked up again, couldn't help it, and caught James turning a page, and thought: *I have a person. I have a few people now*. And then he looked back at his problem set and kept working, because the moment didn't seem to require anything more than that.

* * *

James, for his part, was easy to be around in a way that Ardy had not anticipated and could not entirely account for.

It wasn't that he was uncomplicated — Ardy had learned enough about him by now to know that wasn't true. There were layers to James Rhys that surfaced occasionally and then submerged again, like something moving beneath still water. The comment on their first run about popularity not meaning anything. The way he sometimes went quiet in a group setting in a manner that was so practiced it looked natural unless you were paying close attention. The fact that he volunteered at the children's literacy program every Saturday morning and had never once mentioned it to anyone on the team — Ardy had found out from Owen, who had found out by accident.

"He doesn't like people making a thing of it," Owen had said, with a shrug that suggested this was simply James, take it or leave it.

Ardy had thought about that for longer than was probably warranted.

What James was, mostly, was present. When he was with you he was entirely with you — not scanning the room, not half-attending, not performing interest while thinking about something else. He looked at you when you spoke. He remembered things. Three weeks after Ardy had mentioned, in passing, that his father had been a jockey, James had asked a specific and thoughtful question about it, and Ardy had found himself talking about his father for ten minutes in a way he almost never did, and afterward had felt not the usual hollow ache but something more like relief.

He didn't examine that either. He was getting very good at not examining things.

But at night, sometimes, before sleep came, he let himself acknowledge — briefly, carefully, the way you might open a window in cold weather just enough to feel the air — that James Rhys was becoming something to him. Not a word for it. Not yet. Just a direction his thoughts moved in when he wasn't managing them. Just a name that his mind returned to, reliably, the way a tongue returns to a sore tooth.

Not because it hurt. That was the thing he hadn't expected.

Because it didn't.

* * *

Mack noticed, of course. Mack noticed everything.

She didn't say much about it — she'd said what she had to say at McGoldrick and she wasn't the type to repeat herself — but occasionally, over Tuesday or Thursday coffee, she would look at him in that way she had and then look away again, and the ghost of a smile would pass across her face like a cloud shadow moving across a field.

He pretended not to notice.
She pretended to believe him.
It was, he thought, a very functional arrangement.

* * *

Chapter Eight — The Other Side of the Glass

James Rhys had a system.

It was not a complicated system, but it was reliable, and he had been running it for long enough that most of the time it didn't feel like a system at all. It felt like just being himself — which was, he supposed, the point.

The system was this: be warm, be present, be interested in people, make them feel seen. Volunteer for things. Show up early. Remember birthdays. Be the person in the room who makes everything slightly easier by virtue of being there. Do all of this genuinely, which was not difficult because he was, in fact, a genuinely warm person who was interested in people and liked making things easier.

And in the space that all of that created — the goodwill, the easy popularity, the simple fact that when you were universally liked nobody looked at you too hard — keep the one true thing about yourself so quiet that even you could sometimes forget it was there.

It had worked, more or less, for as long as he could remember.

He was twenty years old and he had never told anyone he was gay. Not out loud. Not in those words. His sister Siobhan knew, or strongly suspected, and they had arrived at a wordless understanding about it that suited them both — she left the door open without making a thing of the door, and he walked through it in his own time, and neither of them discussed the door itself. It was, he thought, a very loving arrangement.

But that was the extent of it. Nobody else. Not his parents, not his teammates, not his friends. Not Owen, who was his roommate and probably his closest friend at USM and who was, James was fairly certain, the least judgmental person he had ever met. Not even Owen.

He told himself this was a choice. He told himself that his sexuality was his own business, that nobody had a right to it, that coming out was a personal decision and not an obligation. All of which was true. He believed all of it.

He also knew, if he was being honest with himself, that the privacy had become something else over the years — not a boundary but a wall, and that somewhere along the way he had lost the ability to tell the difference.

* * *

He had not been prepared for Ardy Alves.

That was the honest truth of it, and James Rhys, whatever else he was, tried very hard to be honest with himself. He had not been prepared. He had met hundreds of people at USM and had processed them all through the system without incident — warm, present, interested, seen — and then Mack MacKenzie had texted him saying come find me at the humanities building second floor after lunch I want you to meet someone and he had gone, because he liked Mack, who was sharp and funny and slightly alarming in the best possible way, and he had turned the corner into that corridor and —

Well.

He'd had crushes before. He knew what they felt like — that particular quality of attention, the way a person could become a fixed point in a room, the way you became aware of exactly where they were without appearing to look. He'd had them on boys since he was thirteen and had become very practiced at managing them. You noticed, you acknowledged to yourself privately that you had noticed, and then you filed it away somewhere safe and got on with your day.

He had filed Ardy away. Several times. With decreasing success.

The problem — if he was going to call it a problem, which some days he wasn't sure was the right word — was that Ardy was not like the other people James had met and folded into his life without incident. Most people, when you turned the warmth on them, opened up like windows in summer. They talked, they laughed, they told you things, they became comfortable and familiar within a few conversations.

Ardy did not do this.

Ardy received warmth with a kind of careful, measuring attention — not suspicious, not unfriendly, but thoughtful, as if he was deciding what to do with it. He gave things back slowly. A sentence at a time. A detail here, a dry observation there, a very occasional almost-smile that arrived without warning and was gone before you could quite look at it directly. He ran like he thought, and he thought like he ran — with a focused economy that wasted nothing, gave nothing away that wasn't intentional.

James found this absolutely riveting — and he had examined that particular fact with considerable care during the long walk back from the stadium on Friday mornings, when he had the cold air and the empty streets to himself.

* * *

They had been running together for three weeks now, Tuesday and Friday mornings, and James had established a rule for himself: the first mile was silence. He'd framed it mentally as giving Ardy space, which was true, but if he was being completely honest it was also about giving himself space. The first mile he could just run, and not have to manage anything, and let the effort and the silence do their work.

The problem was that silence with Ardy was not, as it turned out, neutral territory.

It was warm. It was companionable. It was — and this was the word that kept arriving no matter how many times James sent it away — comfortable. Running beside Ardy in silence felt like something he hadn't felt in a long time, something he wasn't sure he'd ever had with another person: the sense of not having to perform anything whatsoever. Just two bodies doing what they were built for, in the same direction, in the same key.

He was getting worse at the filing system.

Last Tuesday Ardy had said, without looking at him, midway through the third lap: "Your form breaks down on the left side when you're tired. Your hip drops." And James had said "I know" and Ardy had said "Dutil mentioned it?" and James had said "My high school coach mentioned it about four hundred times" and Ardy had made a small sound that was not quite a laugh but close enough that James felt it land somewhere close to his heart and stay there.

He had thought about that small sound, that almost-laugh, with an embarrassing frequency in the days since.

* * *

Owen noticed something was up, because Owen noticed everything and said almost nothing, which was what made him both an excellent roommate and occasionally a liability.

"You're doing the thing," Owen said one evening, not looking up from his laptop.

James, who had been staring at the same paragraph of his education theory textbook for approximately fifteen minutes, looked up. "What thing?"

"The thinking-about-something-but-pretending-not-to thing." Owen turned a page. "You go very still. Like a dog that's heard a sound."

"That's a deeply unflattering comparison."

"Is it wrong?"

James looked back at his textbook. "I'm just thinking about my essay."

Owen said nothing. This was the most eloquent response available to him and he deployed it expertly.

"There's a guy on the track team," James said, after a moment, because the alternative was continuing to stare at the same paragraph. "A freshman. We've been running together."

"Ardy," Owen said.

James looked at him. "How do you know his name?"

"You've mentioned him." Owen's eyes did not leave his laptop. "Four times in the last week. Which is four more times than you usually mention anyone."

James opened his mouth and closed it again. He looked at his textbook. The paragraph looked back at him, unhelpfully.

"He's a good runner," he said finally.

"Clearly," said Owen.

James chose not to pursue this line of conversation. He looked back at his textbook and, this time, actually read the paragraph. Or looked at it, at any rate. The words were there. He was fairly certain of that much.

* * *

He called Siobhan on Sunday, the way he did most Sundays. He waited until Owen headed out for dinner with some friends from his economics class — see you later, don't forget we're out of coffee — and then sat on the floor of his room with his back against the bed and the window showing the gray November sky, and called her.

She was twenty-three and lived in Providence and worked for a small architecture firm and was, in James's estimation, one of the three or four genuinely good people the world had managed to produce. She answered on the second ring.

"How's Portland?" she said.

"Cold."

"It's November in Maine. Was that a surprise?"

"A little, yeah."

She laughed. Then: "How are you?"

This was always the real question, with Siobhan. Not how's school, how's the team, how are your grades — just how are you, with a weight to it that meant she actually wanted to know.

He leaned his head back against the bed. "I'm okay," he said. "There's — " He paused. "I've been running with someone. A freshman. He's — " He stopped again, not sure what he'd been going to say.

Siobhan waited. She was good at that.

"He's interesting," James said finally. "He doesn't say much. But when he does it's always the right thing." He paused. "He makes me want to say the right things too."

There was a brief silence on the line.

"James," Siobhan said, gently.

"I know," he said.

"Okay," she said. And that was all. Just: okay. The door, open. The light on inside.

He looked at the gray November sky for a while after they hung up.

Then he picked up his phone and typed: *Running Friday. 6am. Dress warmer than last time, it's supposed to drop overnight.*

He looked at the message for a moment.

Then he sent it.

* * *

Chapter Nine — The Library

It was Mack's fault, technically.

Though if James had been asked, honestly, what had been occupying his thoughts in the days before that particular Saturday, it would not have been Mack.

It would have been Friday morning's run. Specifically: the moment somewhere in the fifth lap when he had eased off the pace slightly — his hip flexor had been complaining since Tuesday and he'd been careful with it — and Ardy had pulled a half stride ahead without noticing, and James had found himself running just behind and slightly to the left, and had become almost immediately aware that this was a problematic position to be in.

Ardy ran in white shorts and a grey long sleeve, and he ran the way he did everything — with a compact, economical grace that wasted nothing. James had watched the clean line of his shoulders, the efficient pump of his arms, and then — briefly, helplessly, in the way that certain things became unavoidable no matter how many times you filed them away — the way the white shorts pulled taut against the compact, unmistakable curve of him with each stride.

He had pushed the pace back up immediately, drawing level again, fixing his eyes on the track ahead.

His hip flexor had not, in fact, been bothering him at all.

He had thought about this with considerable private mortification for approximately the rest of the day.

* * *

Mack had been the one to mention, on a Thursday morning in late November, that the Portland Public Library had a Saturday reading program for kids who struggled with literacy, and that it was, in her words, "genuinely moving and you should go sometime, not to volunteer necessarily, just to see it, because it will restore whatever faith in humanity you have left after a week of differential equations."

Ardy had filed this away without comment, the way he filed most things Mack said — carefully, for later examination.

Saturday came. He had no practice, no plans, and three hours before he'd promised his mother he'd help her hang curtains in the living room. He told himself he was just going to the library to find a book. He told himself this with a straight face and almost believed it.

* * *

The Portland Public Library on Monument Square was a modern, sleek building, light-filled and open, the kind of place that took its work seriously without being unwelcoming about it. Ardy pushed through the front door and stood for a moment in the entrance hall, getting his bearings.

The children's section was on the ground floor, visible through a wide entrance to the left — bright rugs, colorful low shelves, small chairs arranged in a semicircle. He could hear a voice from somewhere inside, calm and unhurried, and a child's voice responding, and then a small burst of laughter.

He told himself he was going to the periodicals room, which was in the opposite direction.

He went left.

He stopped just inside the archway, far enough back that he wasn't intruding, and looked.

There were six children, ranging in age from perhaps seven to eleven, sitting in the semicircle of small chairs with books open in their laps. A couple of other volunteers were working one-on-one with kids at a low table nearby. And in the center of the semicircle, sitting in a small chair that was genuinely too small for him and somehow not ridiculous, was James.

He was reading aloud. A large picture book, held open and angled to the side so the children could see the illustrations — a dragon, brilliantly colored, mid-flight across a twilit sky — while James read the sparse, large-print words along the bottom of each page. He was doing the voices. Not in an over-the-top way, but subtly, with just enough differentiation between characters that you could follow who was speaking without it becoming a production. The kids were completely still, which Ardy understood was essentially a miracle.

He turned a page, showed the illustration — the dragon landing, wings spread, enormous — and then stopped on a word, pointing to it with one finger.

"This one," he said. He drew it out, breaking it apart like something to be savored. "FORM — id — able." He looked around the semicircle. "Who knows it?"

Silence. One girl raised a tentative hand.

"Chloe."

"Formidable?" she said, uncertain on the last syllable.

"Formidable," James confirmed, and his face did the thing — that open, genuine warmth — and Chloe sat up about half an inch straighter in her chair. "Do you know what it means?"

She shook her head.

"It means something so impressive it's a little bit scary." He looked back at the page, then at the group. "Which fits, because this dragon is about to do something formidable." He glanced around the semicircle with a small smile. "Ready?"

Six heads nodded.

He read on.

Ardy stood in the archway and watched and was very careful not to think about anything in particular, which was becoming his primary occupation whenever James was involved. He noticed the way James's voice dropped instinctively lower at the tense moments in the story, pulling the kids forward without their realizing it, and he watched James tilt the book a little further toward a child on the end who was straining to see — a small, automatic adjustment, made without breaking the flow of the reading, without making anything of it. He watched a small boy in the front row lean forward incrementally with each page, pulled in by some invisible thread, and he watched James notice this and smile to himself, privately, not performing it for anyone.

That was the thing. That private smile. It was the same quality of unguarded he'd heard in James's voice on their runs, in that first mile of silence — the James that existed when he wasn't being watched.

Except that Ardy was watching. And James didn't know.

He should go. He knew he should go. He'd been standing in this archway for — he checked, quietly — eleven minutes, which was well past the point of casual and deep into something he didn't want to examine the name of.

He turned to leave.

"Ardy."

He stopped.

He turned back. James was looking directly at him from the center of the semicircle, the book still open in his hands, six small faces now also turned toward the archway with frank and unselfconscious curiosity.

"Hi," Ardy said. His voice came out level. He was getting very good at that.

James's expression was — it was hard to read, actually. Surprised, certainly. But not displeased. Something that might have been warmth, or might have been the particular expression of someone who has just caught you doing something they find, unexpectedly, rather nice.

"I'll be done in about twenty minutes," James said. "If you wanted to wait."

It wasn't quite a question. Ardy stood there for a moment, very aware of six children staring at him with the open assessment that only children and Mack were unselfconscious enough to deploy.

"Sure," he said. "I'll find a book."

He went to the periodicals room after all, and sat at a table by the window, and looked at a copy of a magazine he didn't read. Twenty minutes passed in a way that felt both very long and surprisingly short. He could hear, faintly, through the building's quiet, the sound of James's voice continuing — the dragon, presumably, doing something formidable.

* * *

James found him there at twelve minutes past eleven, coat on, bag over his shoulder, slightly pink in the cheeks from the warmth of the children's room.

"Hey," he said.

"Hey."

He sat down across the table, uninvited but not unwelcome, and pulled off his scarf. "I didn't know you came here."

"I don't, usually," Ardy said. "Mack mentioned it."

"Mack mentions a lot of things."

"She does."

James looked at him for a moment, and there was something in his expression that was different from his usual easy openness — something quieter, a little more careful. "How long were you standing there?" he asked.

Ardy considered lying. Decided against it. "A while."

James nodded slowly. He looked at the table, then back up. "I don't — " He paused. "I don't usually tell people about this."

"I know. Owen told me. By accident."

Something shifted in James's face. "Of course he did." But it wasn't said with irritation — more a kind of resigned affection. He was quiet for a moment. "What did you think?"

Ardy looked at him. He thought about the small boy leaning forward in his chair. He thought about Chloe and the word formidable and the half inch she'd grown when James said her name. He thought about the private smile.

"I think," he said carefully, "that you're good at a lot of things you don't talk about."

James looked at him for a long moment. The library was quiet around them — the particular hushed quality of Saturday mornings in public buildings, the world outside going about its weekend while in here everything was still and warm and full of the particular calm of a place devoted to good things.

Then James blushed. Clean and sudden, the color rising in his fair cheeks before he could stop it, the winter light falling through the library windows and catching the strawberry gold of his hair, and Ardy found it genuinely difficult to look away, which was becoming less and less surprising. Ardy looked away first. James, a beat later, did the same.

"Coffee?" James said, after a moment. "There's a place on Exchange Street. They actually know what they're doing."

"Sure," Ardy said.

They put on their coats and walked out into the pale December cold together, and neither of them said anything for half a block, and it was, as always, a very comfortable silence.

* * *

Chapter Ten — Exchange Street

The place James had in mind was a narrow storefront on Exchange Street called Coastal Grounds, wedged between an art gallery and a shop that sold nautical antiques. It was the kind of coffee shop that took its work seriously without being pretentious about it — bare brick walls, a long wooden counter, the smell of something roasting in the back, and a chalkboard menu written in the careful hand of someone who genuinely cared what you thought of their single origin Ethiopian.

James held the door. Ardy went in.

They ordered at the counter — James with the focused consideration of someone making an important decision, Ardy with the mild amusement of someone watching him do it — and took their cups to a small table by the window that looked out onto the cobblestones of Exchange Street, wet and gleaming in the December cold.

For a moment neither of them said anything. Outside a couple walked past arm in arm, heads bent against the wind. A gull landed on a cobblestone, looked around with the particular contempt of Portland gulls, and left.

"So," James said.

"So," Ardy said.

James set his cup down and turned it slowly on the table — and Ardy noticed this, the way he noticed everything about James now, with a helpless, precise attention he had mostly given up trying to govern — and looked out the window for a moment before looking back.

"Can I ask you something?"

"Sure."

"Why did you stay? At the library." He said it without any edge to it, genuinely curious. "You could have just left when you saw me. I wouldn't have known."

Ardy considered this honestly. "I don't know," he said. "I think I just — " He looked at his coffee for a moment. "I wanted to see."

"See what?"

"You. Doing that." He paused. "You're different there."

James looked at him. "Different how?"

"Quieter," Ardy said. "More — " He searched for the word. "More yourself, maybe. Than at practice or in the dining hall." He looked up. "I don't know if that makes sense."

James was very still for a moment. Then: "It makes sense."

They drank their coffee. The window was beginning to fog slightly at the edges from the warmth inside, and the street beyond had the soft, slightly unreal quality of a December Saturday — unhurried, muffled, the city in a different gear than the week.

"Can I ask you something now?" Ardy said.

"Fair."

"Why do you do it? The reading program." He held up a hand slightly. "I'm not asking to make a thing of it. I'm just — curious."

James looked at his cup for a moment. "I had trouble reading when I was young," he said. "Not severely, but enough that it was — hard. For a while I thought I was just stupid." He said this without self-pity, plainly, the way you state an old fact that has long since lost its sting. "There was a teacher. She stayed after school with me twice a week for a whole year. She didn't make a big deal of it, didn't treat me like I was broken. She just — sat with me and read with me and made it feel like something we were doing together rather than something wrong with me." He paused. "I just think about her sometimes. When I'm there."

Ardy looked at him across the small table. The coffee shop's warm interior threw a soft glow across James's face. He was, Ardy thought, almost unreasonably beautiful when his guard was down — the light catching the line of his jaw, the curve of his mouth, the way he was leaning slightly forward across the small table as if drawn in by his own story, close enough that Ardy was aware of the warmth of him even across that short distance.

He made himself look at his coffee.

"She sounds like a good teacher," he said.

"She was." A pause. "I want to be a good teacher."

"You will be," Ardy said. And he meant it so directly, with so little qualification, that James looked at him for a moment with an expression Ardy couldn't quite read — something open and a little startled, as if he hadn't expected to be believed so simply.

Then it passed, and James picked up his cup, and outside the gull came back and reconsidered the cobblestones.

"Tell me about your dad," James said. "You mentioned he was a jockey."

Ardy was quiet for a moment. This was not a subject he opened easily, but James asked it the way he asked everything — with a genuine, unhurried interest that made the question feel safe rather than intrusive.

"Benny," he said. "That's what everyone called him. He was small — smaller than me, even — which is how he ended up racing. But he was — " He paused, finding the words. "He was one of those people who took up more space than his size suggested. You know? He was loud, and funny, and he loved horses like some people love — " He stopped. Started again. "He just loved them. You could see it. He'd talk to them before a race like they were old friends he hadn't seen in a while."

James was watching him with that complete attention — not interrupting, not filling the silences, just there.

"He died five years ago," Ardy said. "Accident at the track. Ruptured spleen." He said it evenly, the clinical words a kind of armor he'd developed over time. "I was thirteen."

"I'm sorry," James said. Not in the rushed, reflexive way people sometimes said it, but slowly, like he meant each word individually.

"Thanks." Ardy looked out the window. "My mom was incredible. Is incredible. She just — held everything together without letting me see how hard she was holding." He paused. "I think that's where I get it from. The not showing things."

He hadn't meant to say that last part. It arrived before he could stop it and sat between them on the small table, quiet and slightly exposed.

James didn't pounce on it. He just nodded, slowly, and looked at his coffee, and said: "I think I know something about that."

And that was all. Just that. But it landed, and they both knew it did, and neither of them looked at the other for a moment, and outside on Exchange Street the December wind moved through the cobblestones and the gull finally gave up and flew away toward the harbor.

"More coffee?" James said.

"Yeah," Ardy said. "Okay."

James went to the counter, and Ardy sat at the small table and looked out at the street and let himself feel, briefly and without commentary, the particular warmth of being known — just a little, just enough — by another person.

It was, he thought, not entirely terrifying.

It was, in fact, almost the opposite.

* * *

Chapter Eleven — Small Hours

Mack threw parties the way she did everything else — with complete commitment and absolutely no regard for convention.

It was the second Saturday of December, the last weekend before finals, and she had commandeered the common room of her dormitory floor with the casual authority of someone who had never once in her life asked permission when she could simply proceed. There were string lights strung along the ceiling, a speaker in the corner playing a playlist that moved between Patti Smith and Sufjan Stevens and occasionally, inexplicably, French café music. There was mulled cider on the windowsill in a pot that smelled of cinnamon and cloves and filled the whole room with something that felt almost aggressively like warmth.

There were perhaps twenty people, which was exactly the right size for a Mack party — large enough to have energy, small enough that you could actually talk to someone.

Ardy arrived at eight, which he knew from experience was twenty minutes after Mack's stated start time and therefore exactly on time. He brought a box of those Portuguese custard tarts from a bakery on Congress Street that his mother had discovered and become mildly obsessed with, because Mack had said *just bring yourself* which he had learned meant bring something good to eat.

"Pastel de nata," Mack said, opening the box with genuine delight. "Ardy. You wonderful person."

"My mom found the place."

"Your mom is also a wonderful person. Tell her I said so." She took one immediately and bit into it and closed her eyes for a second. "Okay. Go. Mingle. I have hosting to do."

He mingled, in his way — which was to say he found a spot near the window with a cup of cider and talked to the people who came to him, which was more than he would have expected. He knew more faces now than he would have three months ago. Marcus from the track team was there, and Owen, James's roommate, who arrived early and stationed himself near the food with the quiet efficiency of someone who had correctly identified the optimal position at a party.

James arrived at eight forty-five.

Ardy knew this without looking at the door, which was the kind of thing he had stopped being surprised by.

He looked at the door.

James came in with a girl — twenty-something, dark-haired where James was fair, with the same clear blue eyes and a confidence in the way she moved that suggested she had never once walked into a room and wondered if she was welcome in it. She was laughing at something James had said, her head tilted back, and James was grinning in the easy unguarded way he almost never did in groups.

This, Ardy understood immediately, was the sister.

Mack materialized from somewhere — Mack always materialized, she had a gift for it — and within approximately ninety seconds of Siobhan's arrival they were deep in conversation in the corner by the speaker, Mack gesturing with her cider cup and Siobhan listening with the bright, focused attention of someone who had just met a person they found genuinely interesting.

James watched this with an expression of fond resignation. Then he found Ardy's eyes across the room.

He made his way over, shedding a coat and a scarf, stopping briefly to say hello to three different people on the way because he was James and that was simply what happened when James moved through a room.

"Hey," he said, arriving.

"Hey." Ardy nodded toward the corner. "Your sister."

"I know." James looked over at Mack and Siobhan, who were now apparently exchanging phone numbers. "That happened faster than I expected."

"Mack doesn't waste time."

"No," James agreed. He helped himself to a cup of cider from the windowsill and stood beside Ardy, both of them looking out at the room for a moment. It was a comfortable position — side by side, not quite facing each other, the party providing a kind of cover. Ardy had noticed that they talked more easily this way, when they were both looking at something else.

"How are you feeling about finals?" James asked.

"Fine. You?"

"Terrified," James said pleasantly. "I have a twelve-page paper on Keats due Monday that is currently four pages and two of those pages are the bibliography."

"It's Saturday night."

"I'm aware."

"And you're at a party."

"Mack is very persuasive." He drank his cider. "Also I needed to stop staring at Keats for a while. He was starting to stare back."

Ardy almost smiled. "What's the paper about?"

"Negative capability." He said it with the weary familiarity of someone who had been living with a concept for too long. "Keats's idea that great writers can exist in uncertainty — in doubt and mystery — without reaching after fact and reason." He paused. "The irony of finding this concept maddening while also being unable to resolve it is not lost on me."

Ardy looked at him. "Existing in uncertainty without reaching after fact and reason," he repeated.

"That's the idea."

"That sounds exhausting."

James laughed — a real one, surprised out of him, and Ardy felt the familiar warmth of it somewhere in his chest. "It really does," James said. "And yet."

And yet. The words settled between them with a weight that neither of them addressed.

* * *

The party thinned gradually, the way good parties did — not all at once but in ones and twos, people drifting off into the December night with their coats and their leftover cider warmth. By ten thirty there were perhaps eight people left, scattered across the common room in the loose, comfortable configurations of a party in its final hour.

Siobhan had detached from Mack and found her way to the couch, where she sat with her legs tucked under her and a cup of tea she'd somehow produced and was talking to Owen, who was apparently her intellectual equal in the department of saying a great deal with very few words.

Mack was in the kitchen doing something with the leftover mulled cider that she claimed would improve it. She had produced, from the depths of her enormous tote bag, a small flask that she declined to identify, and was adding measured amounts of its contents to the pot with the focused expression of someone conducting a serious experiment.

James and Ardy had migrated, gradually and without discussion, to the window seat at the far end of the common room — a wide sill with a worn cushion, looking out over the dark campus below, snow beginning to fall in soft, unhurried flakes. They sat at angles to each other, backs against opposite walls, knees not quite touching in the middle.

"Can I ask you something?" Ardy said.

"You keep asking if you can ask things," James said. "You can always ask things."

"Your dad," Ardy said. "You mentioned him once. That he was difficult."

James was quiet for a moment. The snow fell past the window, each flake briefly lit by the light from inside before disappearing into the dark below.

"He's not a bad person," James said carefully. "He's just — he has a very clear idea of what things should look like. His kids, his family, his life." A pause. "I don't always fit the picture."

"In what way?"

James looked at his cup for a moment. "In most ways, I fit fine. I'm good at school, I run track, I'm going to be a teacher which he thinks is noble if not particularly ambitious." He said this without bitterness, just noting it. "But there are things about me that I think he suspects. And that I think he has decided not to suspect, because it's easier." He glanced at Ardy. "Does that make sense?"

Ardy held his gaze for a moment. "Yes," he said quietly. "It makes complete sense."

Something passed between them — not words, not yet, nothing so defined as that. Just a recognition. The particular relief of being understood by someone who understands from the inside.

James looked back out at the snow. "Siobhan's the only one who really — " He stopped. "She just lets me be what I am. Without making a production of it."

"She seems like a good person."

"She's the best person." He said it simply, with a conviction that left no room for qualification.

Ardy thought about his mother. About the way she looked at him sometimes — with that warm, unhurried patience, as if she was waiting for him to arrive somewhere she could already see. The words he hadn't said to her yet, that he could feel gathering inside him, heavier and more inevitable with each passing week. He thought about what it might feel like to say them out loud to another person. Not his mother, not Mack.

Someone like James.

He didn't say any of this. But he thought it, there in the window seat with the snow falling past the glass and the party winding down around them and James's knee almost touching his in the middle of the cushion.

"My mom is like that," he said instead. "The letting me be what I am thing."

James looked at him. And again — that recognition, that quiet, careful thing that passed between them when they got close to the edges of what they were willing to say.

"You're lucky," James said softly.

"I know," Ardy said. "I know I am."

From the kitchen Mack appeared, triumphant, with a jug of what she claimed was improved cider. "Right," she announced to the room. "Who wants some? And before anyone asks — yes, it's better. I don't make mistakes."

The room laughed, and the moment released itself gently, like a breath held too long, and Ardy took a cup of the improved cider and James took a cup of the improved cider, and they both tried it, and it was — whatever Mack had added from that flask — considerably better. They sat in the window seat a little longer while the snow came down outside, and neither of them moved to close the distance between their knees.

But neither of them moved to open it, either.

* * *

Chapter Twelve — Almost

The indoor meet was at Bowdoin.

It was the second Saturday of January, the semester barely a week old, and the world outside the van windows was the particular gray-white of a Maine winter that had settled in and intended to stay. Ardy sat three rows back from James, which was the right distance — close enough to be aware of him, far enough to not have to manage it — and watched the snow-covered fields go by and thought about his race.

The eight hundred. Two laps of the indoor track, the event that suited him best — long enough to require strategy, short enough to demand everything. Coach Dutil had been working with him on his opening two hundred, keeping him from going out too fast, saving something for the bell lap when everyone else was dying.

Trust your fitness, Dutil had said at Thursday's practice. *You're in better shape than you think you are.*

Ardy had nodded and not said what he was thinking, which was that he was aware of exactly what shape he was in, thank you, and that the problem was never fitness. The problem was the space between knowing what you were capable of and allowing yourself to do it.

He looked out the window. Three rows up, James's ginger head was bent over something — a book, probably, he always brought a book on away trips — and Ardy looked at the back of his neck, the short hair there, and then looked back out the window.

Trust your fitness.

* * *

Bowdoin's athletic facility smelled of rubber and effort and the particular electric anticipation of a meet day. The Huskies arrived in their navy and gold, and there was the familiar organized chaos of kit bags and spikes and the sound of a field event already underway somewhere in the building. Ardy changed in silence, laced his spikes with the double knot he always used, and went to find a stretch of floor to warm up on.

James found him there ten minutes later, already mid-routine, and dropped down beside him without a word and began his own warm-up. They worked in silence for a while — the companionable, focused silence of meet day, which was different from the silence of their morning runs, sharper and more inward.

"How are you feeling?" James asked, mid-hip-flexor stretch.

"Good," Ardy said.

"Yeah?"

"Yeah." He paused. "You?"

"Nervous," James said, which surprised Ardy — James rarely admitted to nerves. "I want to go under four today. Really under four." He said it quietly, almost to himself. "I've been close. I want to actually do it."

Ardy looked at him. "You will," he said.

James glanced at him sideways. "You don't know that."

"I've been watching you run for three months," Ardy said. "You will."

Something shifted in James's expression — that brief, open thing, quickly managed. He looked back at his stretch. "Okay," he said. "Okay."

70

Ardy's heat went off at eleven forty.

He had drawn lane three, which suited him. He stood at the line and shook out his arms and breathed — slow in, slow out — and found the place he always looked for before a race, that particular mental stillness where everything unnecessary fell away and there was only the track and his body and what he was about to ask of it.

The gun went.

He ran the first two hundred controlled, exactly as Dutil had drilled him, letting the field set the pace, sitting in third place around the first bend and keeping something in reserve. The indoor track was tight and loud, the crowd noise bouncing off the low ceiling, and he tucked in behind the leader and waited.

Waited.

The bell rang for the final lap and he felt the shift in the field — the slight surge from the front, the panic from the back — and he moved. Not a sprint, not yet, just a controlled acceleration through the back straight, moving up on the outside, and then off the final bend he opened up completely, his lungs burning wide and clean, his legs finding a gear he hadn't been sure was there until this exact moment —

He crossed the line in 1:52.4.

He didn't know this yet. He slowed to a jog, hands behind his head, and tried to find his breath, and heard Dutil somewhere to his left saying something he couldn't make out over the noise.

Then the time went up on the board.

1:52.4. A personal best by almost two seconds.

He stood there for a moment, breathing hard, and felt something he didn't entirely have a word for — not just the satisfaction of a good race but something bigger and less familiar. A sense of himself as capable of more than he'd allowed. He thought about what Dutil had said. *You're in better shape than you think you are.*

Maybe, he thought. Maybe that was true about more than running.

* * *

James's mile was the penultimate event of the day.

Ardy had changed back into his warm-ups and found a spot in the stands and sat with Marcus and Owen — who had come to watch, which was typical Owen, quiet and loyal — and watched James line up in lane two with seven other runners.

He looked composed. Ardy knew by now that this was not the same as being calm.

The gun went, and James went with it — not leading, sitting in the pack, running the first lap well within himself. Ardy watched his form — the long, controlled stride, the slight hip drop on the left that he'd been working on all semester, better now, nearly gone — and felt the particular tension of watching someone you cared about do something that mattered to them.

The bell lap.

James moved at the bell — a long, smooth surge that cut through the field with a clarity that made Ardy sit forward slightly — and came off the final bend with thirty meters to go in second place, and then he was past the leader with twenty meters to go and there was nothing left between him and the line —

3:58.7.

The stands around Ardy made noise and Ardy made noise too, which was not something he did at track meets,

and Owen beside him said "there it is" in his quiet way, and
Marcus said something considerably louder that Ardy
didn't catch.

On the track below, James slowed to a walk, hands
on his knees, head down. Then he straightened and looked
up at the board.

3:58.7.

Ardy watched him take it in. Watched the moment
pass across his face — disbelief first, then something that
was too big to be just happiness, something that reached
back into years of work and doubt and early mornings and
a hip that dropped on the left — and James pressed both
hands briefly over his face and then took them away and
blinked, and his eyes were bright.

He blushed. Even from the stands Ardy could see it
— the color in those fair cheeks, the particular flush of
someone feeling too much to manage it, and this time there
was nothing to will away because the whole field had just
seen James Rhys go under four minutes and he was
allowed to feel whatever he felt.

Ardy was aware that he was smiling. He made no
effort to stop.

* * *

Afterward, in the corridor outside the changing
rooms, the Bowdoin facility beginning to empty around
them, Ardy found James before James found him.

"3:58," Ardy said.

James turned. He was still flushed, his hair damp at
the temples from the race, and he looked — Ardy filed this
away without comment — extraordinary. There was no
more precise word for it.

"3:58," James confirmed. He said it like he was still deciding whether to believe it.

"I told you."

"You told me." James looked at him for a moment, and something in his expression was different from usual — less managed, the filters turned down by the adrenaline and the emotion and whatever it was that a personal best did to a person's defenses. "How did your eight hundred go? I didn't get to see it."

"1:52.4."

James's eyes widened. "That's a PR."

"Yeah."

"By how much?"

"Almost two seconds."

"Ardy." He said it quietly, just the name, with a weight to it. "That's — that's really good."

"So is 3:58."

They stood in the corridor and looked at each other, and the building moved around them — voices, footsteps, the distant clatter of equipment — and none of it touched them particularly. The adrenaline of the race was still in Ardy's blood and he was aware, with a helpless and precise clarity, of exactly how close they were standing. Close enough to see the individual freckles across the bridge of James's nose. Close enough that James's scent — that clean, warm thing, cut grass and something warmer underneath — was present and unmistakable.

James's eyes were very blue.

Ardy was aware of all of this the way you were aware of standing at the edge of something high — not afraid, exactly, but conscious of the drop, the distance, what it would mean to step forward.

James opened his mouth slightly, as if he was going to say something.

He didn't say it.

Whatever it was, it moved across his face and then it was gone, and he looked down for a moment, and when he looked back up the filters were back, gently, carefully, and he said: "The van leaves at four."

"I know," Ardy said.

"Okay." A beat. "Good running today, Ardy."

"You too, James."

James picked up his kit bag and headed back toward the changing room, and Ardy stood in the corridor and watched him go and let himself stand at the edge of that high place for just another moment before stepping back.

* * *

He sat alone on the van on the way home.

Not three rows behind James this time — further back, the last row, the dark window beside him showing nothing but the passing lights of the highway. Around him the team talked and laughed and came down gradually from the high of the day, and Ardy sat with his headphones in and no music playing and looked at the dark window and thought about blue eyes and freckles and a mouth that had opened and not said whatever it was going to say.

He thought about 1:52.4, and what Dutil had said about being in better shape than you thought. He thought about negative capability — existing in uncertainty without reaching after fact and reason — and whether that was wisdom or just a very elegant name for fear.

He didn't sleep on the way home.

He doubted James did either.

****

Chapter Thirteen — The Break

It started the following Tuesday.

Ardy arrived at the stadium at six, the way he always did, and James was not there.

He waited five minutes, which was longer than he usually waited for anything, and then ran alone. Eight laps, his usual Tuesday distance, and the running was fine — his body didn't know the difference — but the silence was different. It had a texture to it that their shared silence never had. It was just quiet. Just cold. Just him.

He checked his phone after. No text. Nothing since Saturday's van ride home, when James had said *good meet today* to the group chat and Ardy had liked the message along with everyone else and that had been that.

He told himself it was nothing. James had slept late, or had an early class, or had simply forgotten.

He told himself this with decreasing conviction over the following days.

* * *

Wednesday, the library. James's usual chair across the table was occupied by someone else — a girl with headphones and a stack of nursing textbooks who had no idea she was sitting in the wrong place. Ardy opened his problem set and worked and did not look at the chair again.

Thursday, the dining hall. James came in with Owen and a couple of guys from the team's five-thousand group and sat at the round table by the window — their table —

but somehow the geometry of it was wrong. He was turned slightly away. He laughed at something one of the five thousand guys said. He was warm and present and easy in the way he always was in groups, and he said hello to Ardy when he sat down, and asked how his problem set was going, and listened to the answer.

But it was the listening of someone going through the motions of attention rather than giving it. Ardy, who had spent a lifetime learning to tell the difference, noticed immediately and said nothing.

Friday morning, no text the night before. Ardy went to the stadium anyway at six and ran alone again and did not check his phone until he got home.

One text, sent at six fourteen. *Sorry — overslept. Next week.*

Ardy read it and put his phone face down on the kitchen table and made coffee and stood at the window looking out at the gray January street and tried to locate, with some precision, what he was feeling.

It was not quite hurt. It was something adjacent to hurt, something that had hurt's shape but was made of a different material — older, more familiar. The particular feeling of having allowed yourself to want something and then been reminded why you'd stopped doing that.

He drank his coffee. He went to class.

* * *

"Something's wrong," Mack said on Thursday.

It was their usual table, their usual coffees, but Mack had closed her book — Sappho today, the same slim volume she'd had in September — and was looking at him with those frank green eyes and the expression she used

when she had decided that pleasantries were not going to
be sufficient.

"I'm fine," Ardy said.

"You're not fine. You've been not fine for a week."
She wrapped both hands around her cup. Then, catching
herself: she shifted, holding it differently, one hand on the
handle, the other flat on the table. "Is it James?"

He looked at his coffee.

"Ardy."

"He's just been — distant," he said. "Since the meet. I
don't know what I did."

"What makes you think you did something?"

"Because things were — " He stopped. "Things were a
certain way. And now they're different. And the only
variable that changed is — " He stopped again.

"The meet at Bowdoin," Mack said quietly.

He looked at her. "You weren't there."

"No. But I know you, and I know him, and I know
what almost looks like." She held his gaze. "Ardy. What do
you think happened?"

"I think — " The words came slowly, each one
considered. "I think maybe he realized something. About —
about what was happening. Between us." He looked at his
coffee. "And I think it scared him. And I think his solution
was to — " He made a small gesture with his hand. Step
back. Close the door.

Mack was quiet for a moment. "Or," she said
carefully, "he's scared of the same things you're scared of.
And the meet at Bowdoin scared him not because of what
he realized about you. But because of what he realized
about himself."

Ardy looked at her.

"I'm not saying I'm right," she said. "I don't know what's going on in James Rhys's head. But I'd be careful about deciding you know the answer before you, like, actually know the answer."

He thought about this. He turned his cup on the table. Outside the McGoldrick windows the January campus was bare and pale, students moving quickly between buildings with their chins tucked, nobody lingering.

"What if I'm right though?" he said. "What if he's — what if knowing what's happening made him not want — " He couldn't finish the sentence.

Mack leaned forward slightly. "Then that's his loss," she said. "And it would hurt, and I would be furious on your behalf, and we would eat a lot of pastel de nata and listen to a lot of Patti Smith until it hurt less." She paused. "But I don't think that's what's happening."

"You don't know that."

"No," she said. "I don't." She picked up her Sappho. "But I know James came to my party and sat in my window seat with you for an hour and a half and neither of you moved an inch further apart than you had to." She opened the book. "That's not someone who doesn't want to be there."

Ardy sat with that for a while. The espresso machine hissed. Someone laughed at a table across the room.

"He hasn't texted," he said finally.

"Text him," Mack said, without looking up.

"I'm not going to text him."

"I know," she said. "You're both going to be very brave and very stupid about this for a while and it's going to be extremely frustrating to watch." She turned a page. "But it will sort itself out."

"How do you know?"

She looked up at him over the top of her book. "Because I'm a witch," she said. "And I don't make mistakes."

He almost laughed. Almost.

* * *

He ran alone that Friday and the Friday after. He studied at the library and James's chair stayed empty. He ate in the dining hall and sometimes James was there and sometimes he wasn't and when he was the warmth was real but the distance was also real and Ardy sat with both of them and said nothing and felt the familiar, practiced weight of wanting something he couldn't reach.

He ran more. He always ran more when things were difficult — longer distances, earlier mornings, the cold air and the empty track and the clean simple arithmetic of effort and distance. It helped, the way it always had, which was to say it helped enough to get through the day without it being the only thing he thought about.

But at night, in the quiet before sleep, he thought about a corridor at Bowdoin and a mouth that had opened and not spoken and blue eyes that had been, for one unguarded moment, entirely unmanaged.

And he thought: maybe Mack was right.

And he thought: maybe she wasn't.

And neither thought helped particularly, which was the thing about uncertainty — it didn't resolve itself just because you were tired of it. It just sat there, patient and unhurried, waiting for something braver than thinking to come along.

* * *

Chapter Fourteen — What Mack Asked

She found him at the library.

Not the public library where the children read about formidable dragons on Saturday mornings — the USM library, third floor, the window overlooking the quad that Ardy had claimed by consistent occupation and that James had taken to using on Wednesday afternoons for reasons he had been careful not to examine.

Ardy wasn't there. James was alone at the table with his Keats and a coffee that had gone cold, and he had been staring at the same page for twenty minutes when Mack materialized in the chair across from him, set down her green tea, and looked at him with those steady, perceptive eyes that he was beginning to understand saw considerably more than was comfortable.

"Hey," he said.

"Hey." She didn't open her book. She just looked at him. "You look terrible."

"Thank you, Mack."

"I mean it kindly. You look like someone who hasn't been sleeping." She tilted her head. "Have you been sleeping?"

"Fine," he said, which was not entirely true. He had been sleeping in the way of someone whose mind had other ideas — going under easily enough and then surfacing at three or four in the morning with a specific and unhelpful clarity about things he'd been trying not to think about.

Mack looked at him for a moment longer. Then: "Can I ask you something?"

"I have a feeling you're going to regardless."

"True." She wrapped both hands around her tea — then shifted, one hand on the handle. A small habit he'd noticed her correcting lately, though he didn't know why. "What are you actually afraid of?"

James looked at her. The library was quiet around them, the third floor always quieter than the rest, the occasional turn of a page or soft footstep the only sounds. Through the window the February quad was iron-gray and empty, a thin skin of old snow on the ground.

"I don't know what you mean," he said.

"I think you do."

He looked at his Keats. Negative capability. He almost laughed.

"Mack — "

"I'm not asking you to tell me anything," she said, and her voice was gentler now, the edge gone from it. "I'm not going to push you somewhere you don't want to go. That's not — " She paused, choosing carefully. "That's not what this is." She looked at her tea. "I just think you're doing the thing where you decide something is impossible before you've actually tested whether it's impossible. And I think it's making you miserable. And I think it's making someone else miserable too." She looked up. "And I think you know all of this already."

James was quiet.

Outside a single student crossed the quad below, moving quickly, coat pulled against the February cold. James watched him go. He thought about Ardy at the library table two weeks ago — the empty chair, Ardy working alone, not looking up when James passed in the corridor. The particular quality of Ardy's not-looking, which was different from ordinary not-looking because

Ardy was always precise about where he directed his attention, and the direction away from James was as deliberate as any direction toward him had ever been.

He had done that. He knew he had done that.

"I'm not — " He stopped. Started again. "It's not simple."

"I know," Mack said. "I'm not saying it's simple."

"There are things — " He looked at his hands on the table. "There are things I haven't said to anyone. That I don't know how to say. That I'm not sure I'm ready to say." He paused. "And I don't think it's fair to — to ask someone else to wait in that space while I figure it out."

Mack was quiet for a moment. Then: "Does the someone else know they're waiting?"

James looked at her.

"Because from where I'm sitting," she said carefully, "it seems like you made that decision for both of you. Without asking." She held his gaze, not unkindly. "And the someone else — who is, by the way, not great at asking for things either, so you two are really something — the someone else would probably, like, prefer to make that decision for himself."

James looked back at the quad. The student was gone.

"What if I get it wrong?" he said. It came out quieter than he intended. More honest.

"Then you get it wrong," Mack said simply. "And it's hard for a while. And then it's less hard." She picked up her tea. "But James — " She waited until he looked at her. "What if you get it right?"

He didn't answer. The question sat between them on the library table, plain and unhurried, in no particular rush to be resolved.

After a moment Mack opened her book — Sappho, the slim volume she carried everywhere — and began to read, and James looked at his Keats and did not read it, and the library went quietly about its business around them, and nobody said anything else.

He thought about her question for three days.

* * *

He thought about it running alone on Tuesday morning, the stadium empty and cold, his breath clouding in the gray pre-dawn air. He thought about it in his education seminar on Wednesday, his pen moving through lecture notes while some other, quieter part of his mind turned the question over and over like a stone in a current. He thought about it Thursday night when Owen was out and the room was quiet and he sat on the floor with his back against the bed and did not call Siobhan because he wasn't ready to say it out loud yet — not even to her.

What if you get it right?

He thought about 1:52.4 on a board at Bowdoin. He thought about Ardy saying *you will* before the mile, flat and certain, as if doubt was simply not a variable he had considered. He thought about the corridor afterward — the way they had stood close enough that Ardy could have counted the freckles across the bridge of James's nose, and how Ardy had not moved away, had not flinched, had stood there steady and present and waiting with the patience of someone who was very good at waiting.

He thought about running beside someone and feeling, for the first time in as long as he could remember, like he didn't have to be anyone other than exactly himself.

On Friday morning he picked up his phone.

He looked at it for a long moment.

Then he typed: *Running tomorrow. 6am. If you want.*

He put the phone down and went to make coffee and tried not to watch the screen. He was approximately thirty seconds from deciding he'd made a terrible mistake when his phone buzzed.

Sure, Ardy had written. *See you there.*

James stood in the small kitchen of his dorm room with his coffee and read the message twice and felt something loosen in his chest that had been tight for three weeks — not gone, not resolved, still complicated and uncharted and frankly terrifying in ways he hadn't fully catalogued yet.

But loosened.

He drank his coffee.

He went to his seminar.

He thought: *okay. Okay.*

* * *

Chapter Fifteen — The Track at Dawn

He was there.

Ardy came through the stadium gate at six and James was already on the track, not running yet, just standing at the start of the straight in his dark training gear with his hands in his pockets and his breath making small clouds in the February air. He looked up when he heard the gate and something in his face did a complicated thing that Ardy couldn't entirely read and didn't try to.

"Hey," James said.

"Hey."

They stood for a moment in the cold and the quiet. The stadium lights were on, throwing their familiar pale wash across the red surface, and beyond the stadium fences Portland was still mostly asleep, the city in that particular suspended state of very early Saturday morning when the night people had gone home and the day people hadn't yet started and the world briefly belonged to no one.

"I owe you an apology," James said.

Ardy looked at him. "You don't — "

"I do." He said it quietly but with a firmness that closed the door on argument. "I pulled back. I know I did. And I didn't explain it and I didn't ask you — " He stopped. Started again. "I just disappeared, basically. And that wasn't fair."

Ardy was quiet for a moment. The cold air moved across the infield in a long, slow wave.

"Okay," he said.

"Okay?"

"Okay." He looked at the track. "You're here now."

James looked at him for a long moment with an expression that was difficult to name — something relieved and careful and a little undone at the edges. Then he nodded. "Yeah," he said. "I'm here now."

They began to run.

* * *

The first mile they didn't talk, the way they never talked in the first mile, and Ardy felt the familiar machinery of it engage — the cold air, the rhythm, the particular mental quiet that running with James produced, which was different from running alone even when they weren't speaking. Something about the presence of him. The way the silence had a shape to it.

He was aware, as he always was now, of James beside him. The long, controlled stride. The clean warm scent of him in the cold air. The sound of his breathing settling into its rhythm.

He was also aware of something different today — a quality of attention coming from James's direction that was different from usual. More deliberate. As if James was working something out, lap by lap, the way Ardy used running to think.

The second mile began.

James said, without looking at him: "Can I tell you something?"

"Yeah," Ardy said.

A long pause. Three hundred meters of it, almost. Ardy didn't rush it.

"I've known something about myself for a long time," James said. His voice was level, his eyes on the track ahead. "Since I was pretty young. And I've spent — a lot of

89

energy, I think, making sure it didn't show. Making sure people saw everything else about me first." He paused. "I'm good at that. Maybe too good."

Ardy ran. He kept his breathing steady and his eyes forward and waited.

"I'm gay," James said. Quietly. Plainly. As if it was something he was trying out in the open air for the first time and finding that it didn't, as it turned out, kill him.

The word went up into the cold morning and hung there for a moment and then dispersed, the way breath did.

Ardy said: "I know."

James looked at him then, a quick sideways glance, surprised.

"I mean — " Ardy kept his eyes on the track. "I didn't know. I suspected." He paused. "In the same way I suspect you suspected something about me."

A beat.

"Yeah," James said. "I did."

They ran another full lap in silence. Not the silence of before — something different now, the air between them slightly changed, as if a pressure had equalized. Ardy could feel his own heartbeat, which was not entirely due to the running.

"I don't have a word yet," Ardy said, on the back straight. "For what I am. I just — I know what I feel. Or what I've been feeling." He glanced sideways. "For a while now."

James was quiet. Then, carefully: "For a while now."

It wasn't a question. Ardy answered it anyway.

"Yeah."

They came around the final bend and into the home straight and neither of them pushed the pace, and the stadium lights threw their long shadows out behind them, and Ardy thought about all the mornings he had run here alone in the dark before any of this had happened, when Portland was just a new city and the track was just a track and the future was just a thing that hadn't arrived yet.

It had arrived. He wasn't entirely sure when.

* * *

They slowed at the end of the straight and walked — the cool-down lap, the way they always did, side by side, not talking for a moment. Ardy's legs felt good. His lungs felt good. Everything, actually, felt surprisingly good for someone who had just said out loud, to another person, in the cold at six in the morning, a thing he had never said out loud to anyone except Mack.

"Does anyone know?" James asked. "About you."

"Mack," Ardy said. "And my mom, I think. She hasn't said anything but — " He paused. "She sees things."

"Mack sees things too."

"Mack sees everything."

"Yeah." A pause. "She came to find me," James said. "At the library. Last week."

"I know." He hesitated. "What did she say?"

James was quiet for a moment. Then: "She asked me what I was actually afraid of."

Ardy looked at him. "What did you tell her?"

"Nothing." He looked back. "But I've been thinking about it since." A beat. "The answer, if you want to know — the honest answer — is everything. All of it. My parents. The team. Being — visible, I suppose. In a way I can't take back." He paused. "And getting it wrong."

"Getting what wrong?"

James looked at him steadily, and the morning light was coming up now at the edges of the sky, the darkness

91

softening to gray, and in that light James Rhys looked
exactly like himself — not the easy public version, not the
carefully managed warmth, but the actual person
underneath all of that, tired and honest and present. His
hair was damp from the run, the longer copper strands on
top falling slightly over his right eye, and Ardy felt the
warm certain glow move through him with a force that had
nothing careful or managed about it whatsoever.

"This," James said simply.

Ardy held his gaze. His heart was doing the thing —
the familiar, inconvenient, no-longer-entirely-unwelcome
thing.

"I don't think you're going to get it wrong," he said.

James looked at him for a long moment. Then that
smile arrived — not the full easy one, not the public one,
but the small private one, the one that didn't necessarily
mean to be seen.

"Okay," he said softly. "Okay."

They finished the cool-down lap and stood at the gate
in the growing light, and the city was beginning to wake up
around them — the first cars, the first birds, the particular
smell of Portland in the early morning, salt and cold and
something that Ardy had stopped thinking of as unfamiliar
some time ago without noticing.

"Same time Tuesday?" James said.

"Same time Tuesday," Ardy said.

James lifted his hand — that small wave — and
headed off toward the campus bridge, and Ardy stood at
the gate and watched him go.

He watched the way James moved in the early
morning light — that long, unhurried stride, the broad line
of his shoulders, the ginger hair catching the first pale gold
of the rising sun — and felt something he could only

describe as warmth, spreading slow and total through his entire body despite the February cold around him. Not the sharp, panicked thing he usually felt and immediately suppressed. Something quieter and deeper and considerably more difficult to close a door on. A tingling that started in his chest and moved outward to his fingertips, his legs, the back of his neck — warm and alive and, he realized with a mild shock, welcome.

He stood there until James disappeared over the bridge.

Then he ran home, and the city was waking up around him, and everything looked, for reasons he couldn't entirely account for, slightly different than it had an hour ago.

* * *

The week that followed was its own particular kind of exquisite difficulty.

They saw each other — at practice, in the dining hall, passing on the campus paths between buildings — and each time Ardy was aware of James with a precision that was new and unguarded, the careful guardedness of the past months loosened by what had passed between them on the track. A glance across the dining hall that lasted a half second longer than necessary. James's hand brushing his shoulder as he passed behind Ardy's chair, light and brief, and the warmth of it staying there long after he'd gone. The particular way James smiled at him now — still the easy public smile, but with something underneath it that was only for Ardy, a small private signal that hadn't existed before Saturday morning.

It was, Ardy thought, both better and considerably harder than not knowing.

He ran every morning. Longer distances than usual, earlier starts, the cold air and the empty track doing their work. He studied. He had coffee with Mack on Tuesday, who looked at him in that way she had — seeing straight through to the thing he wasn't saying — and said nothing whatsoever and was, he thought, very restrained about it.

At night, in the quiet before sleep, he thought about the track at dawn and James's voice saying *I'm gay* into the cold air, plain and careful, like something being set down after a long time of being carried. He thought about the small private smile. He thought about broad shoulders catching the early light, and warmth spreading to his fingertips in the February cold, and the word *this* said simply, meaning everything.

Tuesday morning could not, he felt, come soon enough.

* * *

Chapter Sixteen — The Championships

The Little East Conference Indoor Championships were held on the last Saturday of February at a facility in Worcester, Massachusetts, and the Huskies traveled down on Friday evening in two vans that smelled of athletic tape and nervous energy and the particular collective focus of a team that had been building toward something for months.

Ardy sat beside James this time.

This had not been discussed. James had simply arrived at the van with his kit bag and looked at the available seats and sat down next to Ardy, and Ardy had moved his bag to make room, and that had been that. Marcus, across the aisle, raised an eyebrow approximately one millimeter and said nothing, which was the correct response.

They talked on the way down — not about the meet, not about anything important, just the easy back-and-forth that had become their particular language over the past months. James had strong opinions about the audiobook Owen had recommended to him, which he described as "aggressively life-affirming in a way I find exhausting." Ardy said he didn't listen to audiobooks. James looked at him as if he had said something genuinely surprising. Ardy explained that he preferred silence when he wasn't reading. James said that tracked completely. Ardy almost smiled.

Outside the van windows the Massachusetts darkness went by, and the team talked and dozed around them, and at some point James fell asleep against the window with his head tilted back and his mouth very slightly open, and Ardy looked at him for a moment — the line of his jaw, his hair catching the light, his head tilted back in the easy way of someone too tired to hold themselves upright, the particular vulnerability of someone asleep — and then looked back at the road ahead and let the miles go by.

* * *

The facility in Worcester was everything Fitzpatrick Stadium was not — vast and loud and fluorescent, the kind of place that announced the seriousness of the occasion through sheer scale. Multiple teams moved through the warm-up areas in their conference colors, and the noise of the place bounced off the high ceiling in a constant, energizing hum.

Ardy changed in silence and found a stretch of floor and worked through his routine with the focused inwardness of meet day. Around him the Huskies moved and talked and prepared, and Coach Dubé walked the warm-up area with his clipboard and the expression of a man quietly confident in his team, stopping occasionally to say something brief and specific to an athlete that sent them back to their warm-up looking slightly taller.

He stopped beside Ardy.

"How are you feeling?"

"Good," Ardy said.

Dubé looked at him for a moment with the evaluating squint Ardy had come to recognize as his version of approval. "You've had a good season," he said. "Today go out and run like you know that." He moved on.

Ardy went back to his warm-up and thought about what Dubé had said, and about what Dutil had said at Bowdoin — *you're in better shape than you think you are*

— and about what James had said on the track at dawn, and about what he himself had said, and about the week since, and the glances across the dining hall, and warmth spreading to his fingertips in the February cold.

He was, he decided, in better shape than he had ever been in his life. In every sense of that.

* * *

His heat went off at eleven fifteen.

Eight hundred meters. Two laps. The event that suited him best.

He stood at the line and found the stillness he always looked for, and the gun went, and he ran.

He ran better than he had ever run.

It was not something he could entirely explain afterward — that quality of a race where everything that was supposed to work worked, where the body and the mind arrived at the same place at the same time and stopped arguing with each other. He ran the first lap controlled and patient, and the bell rang, and he moved — not with desperation but with a clean, certain authority, like someone who had decided something and was simply following through on the decision — and came off the final bend with his legs on fire and his lungs open wide and crossed the line in first place.

1:50.1.

He stood with his hands on his knees and breathed and heard the number go up and felt something move through him that was enormous and quiet at the same time, the way the biggest things sometimes were.

First place. A personal best by over two seconds. A time that would, he would learn later, stand as the top performance in the eight hundred at the LEC Indoor Championships that year.

He found James in the warm-up area afterward, still preparing for the mile, and James took one look at his face and said "tell me" and Ardy told him and James's face did the complicated, unguarded thing it did when he felt too much to manage, and he put his hand on Ardy's shoulder and squeezed once, briefly, and said "I knew it" and Ardy felt the warmth of his hand through the thin fabric of his singlet and said nothing and looked at the floor and was very grateful for the noise of the facility around them.

* * *

James's mile was the final distance event of the day.

By then Ardy had changed back into his warm-ups and found a spot in the stands between Mack — who had driven down with Siobhan that morning, because of course she had — and Owen, who was eating a granola bar with the composed efficiency of someone for whom athletic competition was primarily a spectator sport.

"How are you feeling?" Mack said, when he sat down.

"About what?"

She gave him a look.

"Fine," he said. "Good. I'm good."

"You ran 1:50," she said. "You can be better than good."

"I'm very good," he said, and she laughed and bumped his shoulder with hers and turned back to the track.

Siobhan, on Mack's other side, leaned forward and caught Ardy's eye. She had James's blue eyes, he noticed, but a different quality in them — warmer, more immediately readable. She smiled at him — a real one, knowing and kind — and he understood, without anything being said, that she knew exactly who he was and was entirely glad he existed.

He looked back at the track.

James was at the line.

Eight runners, navy and gold among them, the particular stillness of the moments before a gun. Ardy watched James shake out his arms, settle his shoulders, find whatever he found before a race. He watched the number on the back of his singlet — 14 — and the ginger hair and the broad shoulders, and then, because he allowed himself such things now, the dark blue fabric of his tight running shorts stretched perfectly over the beautiful curve of his backside. And Ardy felt the warm certain glow that had become simply the texture of his daily life.

The gun went.

James ran beautifully. There was no other word for it — he ran with that fluid, unhurried economy that Ardy had been watching since September, the long stride eating up the track, and he sat in the pack through the first lap and a half and then moved at the bell with the clean decisive authority of someone who had been waiting for exactly this moment.

He came off the final bend in second place.

He crossed the line in first.

3:56.4.

The stands around Ardy erupted and Ardy was on his feet without knowing he'd stood up, and Mack beside him was making a noise that was somewhere between a cheer and a war cry, and Siobhan had both hands over her mouth, and Owen said "there it is" again in his quiet way, and on the track below James slowed to a walk and looked up at the board and stood very still for a moment.

3:56.4. A LEC Championship. A personal best by more than two seconds.

He looked up into the stands, and Ardy didn't know how, in that loud and crowded facility, James found him as quickly as he did — but he did. Those clear blue eyes finding him across the distance, and James's face doing the thing, the unmanaged thing, the flush the color rising in his cheeks and his eyes bright with something that was more than the race.

Ardy held his gaze across the stands and the noise and the distance.

He did not look away.

* * *

Afterward, outside the facility in the cold Massachusetts night, waiting for the rest of the team to load the vans, Ardy and James stood apart from the group in the way they had learned to do — not conspicuously, just slightly, just enough.

"3:56," Ardy said.

"1:50," James said.

They looked at each other.

"Good day," James said.

"Yeah," Ardy said. "Good day."

The cold Massachusetts air moved between them and the parking lot was washed in the amber glow of overhead lights, their shadows stretching long across the asphalt behind them. and somewhere nearby their teammates were laughing about something and the night was cold and clear and full of stars, and James's shoulder was warm against Ardy's in the dark.

Neither of them moved away.

* * *

On the van home James fell asleep again, and this time his head came to rest, gradually, against Ardy's shoulder — not dramatically, just the slow drift of someone too tired to hold themselves upright, the most natural thing in the world.

Ardy sat very still.

He looked out the window at the dark highway and the passing lights and felt the weight of James's head against his shoulder and the alluring warmth of him — that particular warmth of another person's body, close and real and faintly scented with the night's effort — and thought about nothing whatsoever, which was, at this particular moment, the same as thinking about everything.

He did not move for the entire ride home.

* * *

Chapter Seventeen — What Ardy Told His Mother

It happened on a Sunday.

Not because Sunday was a particularly significant day, not because Ardy had planned it or chosen it or worked up to it with any deliberate intention. It happened because it was a Sunday evening in early March and his mother had made caldo verde — the Portuguese soup his father had loved, that she made when she missed him. It filled the small apartment on Brackett Street with the aroma of kale and chouriço and something that was not quite sadness but lived in the same neighborhood — and they were sitting at the kitchen table after dinner with their tea, and the apartment was quiet, and Annie looked at him with that expression she had.

The one that meant she was waiting. That she could see where he was going even if he hadn't started walking yet.

He looked at his tea.

"Mom," he said.

"I know, baby," she said.

He looked up.

She was watching him with those deep brown eyes that had seen everything and kept it all safe — his childhood, his father's death, every silent car ride and early morning and late night that had made up the years since. She looked tired in the way she always looked after a long shift, but underneath the tiredness was something steady and warm and completely certain.

"I haven't said anything yet," he said.

"I know," she said again. Gently. "Take your time."

He looked back at his tea. He turned the mug in his hands — both hands, the warmth of it against his palms — and thought about all the times he had sat at this table or a table like it and felt the words gathering and pushed them back down, and thought about how tired he was of pushing, and thought about James on a track at dawn saying *I'm gay* into the cold air plain and simple like something being set free.

"I think I'm gay," he said. "Or — I don't know exactly what the word is yet. But I know what I feel." He paused. "I know who I feel it for."

The kitchen was very quiet. Outside the window the March wind moved through the street, and somewhere below a car passed, its headlights sweeping briefly across the ceiling.

Annie reached across the table and put her hand over his.

"I know, baby," she said, for the third time. And then: "I've been waiting for you to be ready to tell me."

Ardy looked at her hand on his. Her nurse's hands, capable and sure, the hands that had held everything together for five years without letting him see the effort.

"How long have you known?" he said.

She considered this honestly. "A while," she said. "Since you were young, maybe. Or I suspected. A mother notices things." She squeezed his hand. "I didn't want to push you anywhere you weren't ready to go."

He thought about Mack saying something very similar. He thought about all the people who had quietly held the door open while he found his way to it in his own time.

"Are you — " he started.

"Ardy." She said his name the way she always said it — the R and the D, his father's invention, worn smooth by years of use. "You are my son. You are the best thing that has ever happened to me. Nothing changes. Nothing has ever needed to change." Her eyes were bright but her voice was steady, the way her voice always was when she meant something completely. "Do you understand me?"

He nodded. He didn't trust his voice entirely.

"Good." She squeezed his hand once more and then sat back and picked up her tea, and the kitchen settled around them — the tick of the radiator, the wind outside, the smell of caldo verde still in the air — and it was, Ardy realized, exactly the same as it had been twenty minutes ago. The apartment was the same. His mother was the same. He was the same.

And also everything was different, in the quiet, total way that things were different when you put down something you'd been carrying for a very long time.

They sat in a comfortable silence for a while. Outside the wind moved through Brackett Street and the March night was cold and clear and the small ceramic lighthouse on the windowsill caught the kitchen light the way it always did, patient and steady.

"There's someone," Ardy said, after a while.

Annie looked at him over her tea, and the corner of her mouth moved. Not quite a smile. The promise of one.

"Tell me," she said.

And so he did.

He started haltingly — looking at the table, turning his mug in his hands, the words coming out in pieces rather than sentences. There was a guy. On the track team. A junior. They'd been running together since October.

Annie said nothing. Just listened.

He's — Ardy stopped. Started again. He's a good runner. Really good. He went sub-four at the LEC Championships last week. And he volunteers at the library on Saturdays, with kids who have trouble reading, because he had trouble reading when he was young and there was a teacher who helped him and he never forgot it. And he's studying to be a teacher himself, secondary school English, and he — he's just —

He stopped again. Looked up briefly, looked back down.

He's kind, Ardy said. Like genuinely kind, not faking it. He remembers things. Three weeks after I mentioned Dad was a jockey he asked a specific question about it. Just — out of nowhere. Because he'd been thinking about it.

Something was happening as he talked. He could feel it — a loosening, a warmth, the words coming a little easier with each one. He looked up at his mother and found he didn't need to look back down quite so quickly.

He's funny too, he said, and heard the surprise of that in his own voice, as if he'd just remembered it. Not obvious funny. Dry. He has these strong opinions about coffee — like genuinely strong, it's slightly ridiculous — and he'll spend a whole lap describing everything wrong with whatever he had that morning and somehow it's just —

He shook his head, almost smiling now.

And there's this thing he does when he's embarrassed or really happy — he blushes, just completely unstoppably, and he hates it, you can see him trying to stop it, but he can't, and it's — Mom, it's the most —

He stopped. He was smiling properly now, a real one, and he looked at his mother across the kitchen table and felt something he hadn't expected at all — not embarrassment, not the careful managed neutrality he'd arrived at the table with, but something open and uncomplicated and almost giddy.

It felt, he realized, like being happy about something. Just that. Just simply happy.

He told her the rest — the locker corridor and Mack's witchcraft, the morning runs and the first mile of silence and the scent of something warm and clean in the cold air. The almost in the corridor afterward. The week of distance and the week of aching and the track at dawn in February when James had said the thing out loud for the first time, plain and simple, like something being set free.

The van home from Worcester, he said. And then quieter, looking at his mug: his head on my shoulder the whole way home.

He looked up.

Annie was watching him with that expression — the one from his first track meet and his graduation and every other moment she had been proud without announcing it. Her tea had gone completely cold.

"He sounds," she said carefully, "like a very good person."

"He is," Ardy said. "He's — yeah. He is."

"Does he know how you feel?"

"More or less." He paused. "We're — it's still — " He searched for the word. "Uncharted."

"Uncharted," she repeated, with a small, warm amusement. "That's one word for it." She looked at him steadily. "Are you happy, Ardy?"

He thought about it. He thought about that incredible warm glow spreading through him in the stands in Worcester. He thought about running beside someone in the early morning dark and feeling, for the first time in as long as he could remember, like he didn't have to be anyone other than exactly himself.

"Yeah," he said. "I think I actually am."

Annie looked at him for a long moment. Then she stood up and came around the table and put her arms around him — briefly, firmly, the way she hugged, no nonsense about it — and he leaned into it the way he had when he was small, and she said nothing, and he said nothing, and the kitchen held them both.

When she stepped back her eyes were wet, which was the first time he had seen that in five years, and he understood that this was not sadness.

"Your dad would have loved him," she said. "Sight unseen. He always loved runners."

Ardy laughed — a real one, sudden and full, the kind that came from somewhere deep and uncomplicated — and Annie laughed too, and the sound of it filled the small kitchen on Brackett Street and went out into the March night, and the ceramic lighthouse on the windowsill stood its steady watch, and somewhere across the city James Rhys was probably asleep, or reading, or lying awake in the quiet before sleep thinking about a certain direction his thoughts kept returning to.

And Ardy, for the first time in as long as he could remember, felt entirely, simply glad to be exactly where he was.

* * *

Chapter Eighteen — The Lean

It was a Saturday in late March, the kind of day that Maine produces occasionally in early spring as a kind of promise — not warm exactly, but softer than winter, the air carrying something tentative and green underneath the cold, the sky a pale, washed blue that suggested the possibility of things.

Ardy had texted James in the morning. Not about running. Just: *Are you around today?*

James had replied within two minutes. *Yeah. Want to walk somewhere?*

They met at the Brackett Street end of the Western Promenade at noon — the long elevated park that ran along the ridge of the West End, looking out over the railroad yards and the Fore River and, beyond that, the distant shimmer of Casco Bay. It was Ardy's favorite place in Portland. He had found it in his first week, running, and had come back to it again and again through the fall and winter, drawn by the particular quality of the view — the way the city fell away below and the water opened up beyond, and you could stand on the ridge and feel, briefly, like the world was larger than whatever was currently occupying your thoughts.

James arrived in a grey jacket and dark jeans, his hands in his pockets, his hair doing something the March wind had opinions about. He looked, as he always looked when he wasn't in his running kit, slightly surprising — like seeing a word you knew well written in a different hand.

"Hey," he said.

"Hey."

They began to walk.

* * *

The Promenade was quiet on a March Saturday — a few dog walkers, a couple with a stroller, an old man on a bench reading a newspaper with the focused determination of someone who had earned the right to sit outside in fifty degree weather and call it pleasant. The bare trees along the path were beginning to show the first faint suggestion of buds, and the view to the south was wide and clear and pale.

They talked as they walked, the easy back and forth that had become their language — James had finished his Keats paper, finally, and received a grade that he described as "honestly more than I deserved given the state I was in." Ardy had a problem set due Monday that he was cautiously confident about. The outdoor season was starting in two weeks and Dutil had been hinting at some new interval work that Marcus had described as medieval.

It was ordinary conversation. Ardy was aware, underneath it, of everything that was not ordinary — the fact of what had been said on the track at dawn, and what had not yet been said anywhere, and James walking beside him close enough that their arms occasionally brushed when the path narrowed, and neither of them stepping away when it happened.

They reached the southern end of the Promenade where a series of benches looked out over the full sweep of the view — the river, the bay, the islands low on the horizon, the late March sky enormous above it all. Ardy stopped at one without really deciding to, and James stopped too, and they sat.

For a moment neither of them spoke. The wind came off the water and the view opened out before them, wide and patient, and below the ridge the city went about its Saturday.

"I told my mom," Ardy said. "About me. About — " He paused. "About you."

James turned to look at him. "Yeah?"

"Yeah." Ardy looked at the water. "A couple of weeks ago. Sunday night." He paused. "She said she already knew."

"Of course she did," James said softly.

"She wants to meet you." He glanced sideways. "Not in a — she's not going to make it weird. She just — she wants to meet you."

Something moved across James's face — something open and a little undone, the way it got when he was caught off guard by something good. "I'd like that," he said. Quietly, meaning it.

They sat with that for a moment. The wind moved through the bare trees along the path and the water below caught the pale light and held it.

"I've been thinking," James said, "about what you said. On the track." He looked at his hands. "That you know what you feel. And who you feel it for."

Ardy's heart was doing the thing. "Yeah," he said.

"I've been thinking about that a lot, actually." He paused. "In case you were wondering."

"I was wondering," Ardy said.

James looked at him then — directly, fully, without the usual careful management, and Ardy looked back, and the March wind came off the water and neither of them said anything for a moment, and it was not an uncomfortable silence but something charged and still, like the air before something changes.

"I don't entirely know what I'm doing," James said. "I want to be honest about that. I've never — " He stopped. "This is new territory for me."

"Me too," Ardy said.

"Okay." James nodded slowly. "Okay. I just — I wanted you to know that whatever this is, I'm — " He paused, looking for the word. "I'm not going anywhere. I'm done going anywhere. The thing I did in January — pulling back — I'm not doing that again."

Ardy looked at him. "Good," he said.

"Good," James agreed.

And then neither of them spoke for a while, and the city moved below them, and the water moved beyond, and at some point — Ardy could not have said exactly when, whether it was him or James or simply the slow inevitable gravity of two people sitting very close on a bench with the world spread out before them — James's shoulder came to rest against his.

Not dramatically. Not announced. Just — there. Warm and solid and present, the way James was always present, and Ardy felt the warmth of it move through him like the first genuinely warm day after a long winter, slow and total and enormously, quietly welcome.

He didn't move.

James didn't move.

They sat like that for a long time, looking out at the water, the islands, the enormous pale sky. Ardy was aware of every point of contact between them — shoulder, upper arm, their body heat gently radiating even through their jackets — and it was the most and least dramatic thing that had ever happened to him, which seemed about right.

After a while James said, very quietly, without moving: "Is this okay?"

"Yeah," Ardy said. Just as quietly. "This is very okay."

He felt rather than saw James's small exhale — the loosening of something held — and then James turned his head slightly, and Ardy turned his, and they were very close, the way they had been in a corridor at Bowdoin in January except that this time neither of them looked away, and neither of them moved back. James's eyes moved over Ardy's face with a quiet, unhurried attention — the tender, dark brown eyes, the smooth tan skin, the particular sweetness of a face that James had been looking at for months and was only now, finally, allowing himself to actually see — and something in James's expression shifted. He looked, for once, like someone who had stopped deciding against something. And James's eyes were that clear impossible blue and there was a single freckle just below his left eye that Ardy had not noticed before and that he thought he would probably remember for the rest of his life.

James leaned in. Slowly, giving him every opportunity to decide.

Ardy closed the last of the distance himself.

The kiss was soft and brief and a little uncertain, the way first kisses were, and it tasted of the cold salt air and something warmer underneath, and when they separated — just an inch, just enough — James was already blushing, the color rising helplessly in his fair cheeks, and Ardy looked at him and felt a laugh rise up from somewhere completely uncomplicated.

Not at James. Never at James. Just — joy. The specific, unexpected joy of something you had wanted for a long time arriving exactly as it should, quietly and without fanfare, on a bench in the West End on a pale Saturday in March.

James saw the laugh and something in his face relaxed entirely, the last of the careful management dissolving, and he laughed too — a soft, slightly disbelieving sound — and shook his head.

"Okay," he said.

"Yeah," Ardy said. "Okay."

They sat on the bench a while longer, shoulder to shoulder, blinking now in the soft sunlight, looking out at Casco Bay and the distant islands and the enormous March sky, and the wind came and went, and below them Portland went about its Saturday, and neither of them said very much, and neither of them needed to.

* * *

Chapter Nineteen — Spring

The first outdoor meet of the season was on a Saturday in late April, at a small college outside of Portland, and the day was everything a Maine spring day occasionally consented to be — clear and bright and genuinely warm, the kind of warmth that felt earned after the long gray of winter, the sky a deep unqualified blue and the trees along the edge of the track in full new leaf, that particular vivid green that only exists for about two weeks a year before settling into the ordinary green of summer.

Ardy stood at the edge of the infield in his white USM singlet and felt the sun on his face and thought: yes. This. This is the right thing.

* * *

They had told almost nobody.

This was a mutual and unspoken decision, arrived at in the way most of their decisions were arrived at — without formal discussion, through the gradual accumulation of small understandings. James was not ready to be visible in that way, not yet, and Ardy understood this completely because he was not entirely ready either, and they had talked about it once, briefly and honestly, and agreed that what they were was theirs for now, and that was enough.

Mack knew, obviously. Mack had known before they did.

Siobhan knew. She had texted Ardy directly the week after the bench — just: *I'm really glad. Take care of him —*

and Ardy had read it three times and replied *I will* and meant it with everything he had.

Annie knew. She had met James for the first time two weeks ago, Sunday dinner on Brackett Street, caldo verde again because it was that kind of evening, and James had arrived with flowers for Annie and a bottle of sparkling water and had spent the first ten minutes being slightly more formal than he usually was, which Ardy found quietly hilarious, and Annie had seen straight through it immediately and said *James, sit down, you're family* and that had been that. James had washed up after dinner without being asked, and Annie had told him the story of how Benny got the name Ardy, and James had looked at Ardy across the kitchen with an expression that Ardy felt somewhere in the center of his chest.

Owen knew, because Owen always knew, and had responded by saying absolutely nothing and buying an extra coffee for Ardy the next morning and leaving it on the library table in front of him without a word, which was the most Owen thing that had ever happened.

For now that was enough. It was, in fact, more than enough. It was everything.

* * *

The meet itself was everything a first outdoor meet of the season should be — slightly chaotic, enormously cheerful, the whole team blinking in the April sunshine like people emerging from a long hibernation, which was more or less what they were.

Ardy ran the eight hundred in the second heat of the morning and won it in 1:51.3, which was not his best time but was clean and controlled and exactly what Dutil had asked for — a fitness check, not a full effort, saving something for the conference season ahead. He came off the track feeling good and loose and found James on the infield and James said "nice" in that quiet way that meant considerably more than nice and touched his arm briefly, just above the elbow, and Ardy felt the warmth of it and said nothing and they stood together in the April sunshine and watched the field events for a while.

James ran the mile in the afternoon, the final event of the day.

By then Mack had appeared in the stands — she had driven over with Siobhan, who was visiting for the weekend, and they were sitting together in the third row with Mack's inevitable book open in her lap, though she appeared to be paying more attention to the track than to Sappho. She was wearing a yellow jacket over her usual dark clothes and had added a streak of yellow to the pink tips of her hair in what she described as "school spirit, interpreted." Siobhan beside her was laughing at something and had James's blue eyes and Annie's ease with the world, and they had become, over the past weeks, something close to their own kind of friends.

Annie was there too.

She had come straight from a shift — still in her scrubs, a thermos of coffee from the Portuguese bakery in one hand, her lanyard still around her neck — and had found Mack and Siobhan without any difficulty, because Ardy had texted her that morning: *look for the girl with the pink hair, you can't miss her*. She had introduced herself with the calm, warm efficiency of a woman who had never once in her life needed a formal occasion to make a friend. She had waved at Ardy from the stands when she arrived and he had waved back and felt something expand in his chest — his mother, his people, all in the same row, the separate parts of his life quietly becoming one thing.

He sat with them between events. Mack handed him half a granola bar without being asked. Annie refilled his water bottle from her thermos bag and squeezed his hand briefly, which was everything. Siobhan asked him intelligent questions about the mile that suggested she had been doing research, which made him like her more than he already did. And Mack and Annie had already, in the forty minutes since they'd met, developed the easy rapport of two people who had been looking after the same person from different directions and recognized each other immediately.

"How's he feeling?" Siobhan asked, nodding toward James on the infield below.

"Good," Ardy said. "He's ready."

She nodded, and looked at Ardy for a moment with those blue eyes, and then looked back at the track. "He's happy," she said quietly. "I just want you to know that. He's — I haven't seen him like this in a long time."

Ardy looked at his water bottle. "Yeah," he said. "Me too."

Mack, who had been pretending to read, said nothing and turned a page.

* * *

The mile went off at four fifteen, the sun lower now and golden, throwing long shadows across the track.

Eight runners. James in lane two, the way he always preferred. Ardy watched him settle at the line and find whatever he found before a race — that stillness, that internal arrival — and felt the warm certain glow that had become, over the past weeks, simply the texture of his daily life. Not overwhelming. Not managed. Just there, the way the sun was there, the way the sound of James's voice was there, the way the first mile of silence on an early morning run was there. Part of the furniture of being alive.

The gun went.

James ran beautifully, the way he always ran beautifully, the long fluid stride unhurried and exact, and he sat in the pack through the first half and then moved at the bell with that clean decisive authority that Ardy had been watching since September and still found, every single time, impossible not to feel.

He crossed the line first.

3:57.2.

The stands made noise and Mack made her war cry and Siobhan pressed both hands over her mouth and Annie said something that was lost in the noise but looked, from the shape of her face, like *yes* and Ardy was on his feet, the way he always was for this, watching James slow to a walk and look up at the board and take it in.

James looked up into the stands.

He found Ardy, the way he always found Ardy, across whatever distance was between them.

He smiled — not the easy public one, not the one for everyone, but the small private one that Ardy had first seen at the public library on a Saturday morning, the one that didn't necessarily mean to be seen. Except that now it did. Now it was entirely, specifically, for Ardy to see.

Ardy smiled back.

* * *

Afterward, when the meet was over and the team was packing up and the golden afternoon was tipping toward evening, Ardy and James walked a slow lap of the track together — not running, just walking, side by side in the long April light, their shadows stretching out behind them.

"Good day," Ardy said.

"Good day," James agreed.

Their hands were close at their sides. Not touching — not yet, not here, not in front of everyone — but close. The distance between them the width of a decision that hadn't quite been made yet but was very nearly there.

"Next week," James said, looking at the track ahead.

"Next week," Ardy said.

They walked on, and the shadows lengthened, and behind them in the stands Mack had returned to her Sappho and Annie was finishing her coffee and Siobhan was laughing at something Owen had said, and the late April sun lay warm and golden across the track, and the trees at the field's edge were that vivid particular green, and the future was open in all directions, wide and uncharted and full of the very best kind of uncertainty.

The kind you ran toward.

* * *

About the Author

Elliot Fife grew up in a small beach town in southeast Massachusetts, not far from the Cape Cod Canal. He spent his adolescence writing stories while quietly observing the handsome surfers, runners, and musicians who gave his little town its sense of possibility. He was the resident geek among his friends — always drawn to the emotional undercurrents of growing up rather than the surface of things.

He now lives and works in New York City, on the Upper West Side of Manhattan. On weekends he writes fiction — mostly queer coming-of-age narratives about the tender complexities of first love, identity, and belonging. Stories about the distance between who we are and who we allow ourselves to become.

Elliot Fife is the pen name he uses because it reminds him of two very lovely guys he once knew.

The First Mile: A Story of Distance and Desire is his debut novella.

* 9 7 9 8 2 3 4 0 5 9 5 5 0 *